The Pugilist's Wife

The Pugilist's Wife

a novel

David Armand

Texas Review Press
Huntsville, Texas

FIRST EDITION
Cover Design by Pattie Steib
Cover Art by Edward M. Alba, Sr.
Author's Photo by Lucy Armand

This is a work of fiction. The characters, incidents, and dialogue are drawn from the author's imagination and are not to be construed as real. Any resemblance to actual events or persons, living or dead, is entirely coincidental.

Requests for permissions to reproduce material from this work should be sent to:

Texas Review Press
English Department
Sam Houston State University
P.O. Box 2146
Huntsville, TX 77341-2146

The author wishes to express his sincere gratitude to Paul Ruffin, Jack Bedell, Kevin Cutrer, Pattie Steib, Dayne Sherman, Tim Gautreaux, Norman German, Ben Pletcher, and the Southeastern Louisiana University Department of English for their invaluable assistance in the publication of this book.

Library of Congress Cataloging-in-Publication Data

Armand, David, 1980-
 The pugilist's wife / David Armand. — 1st ed.
  p. cm.
 ISBN 978-1-933896-67-0 (pbk. : alk. paper)
 1. Man-woman relationships—Louisiana—Fiction. 2. Louisiana—Fiction. I. Title.
 PS3601.R55P84 2011
 813'.6—dc22

                        2011023206

Printed in the United States of America

The Pugilist's Wife

The Lord shall make the rain of thy land powder and dust: from heaven shall it come down upon thee, until thou be destroyed.

Deuteronomy 28:24

August 27 1987

Magdalene

A band of clouds rolls in overhead like horses thundering but brings with it no rain. It's summer. And the hot August air wraps itself around the woods and town that is surrounded by them like a damp wool blanket. It hangs between trees and around cars and houses, making everything feel stale and stagnant, bloated with heat. The leaves and grass are dry and turning a sharp yellowbrown. The small crops are beginning to die and the folks in town are losing hope that the rain will come in time to save what is left. It is all over. Everywhere this feeling of death, dryness, loss of hope.

It's been four months since the last rain and the small yard around Magdalene's house has dried up and is now dusty and brown. The grass is clumped in small dry patches that wilt under the dust and the sun. A breeze occasionally stirs up little twisters of dirt and hay that snake across the yard, turning into clouds of dust which then settle on the ground and the dead dry grass. But what is needed and is being prayed for by everyone is a good rain to soak up this dust, to get into the soil and revive the sick and thirsty earth.

Ever since the drought began sometime mid-April, Magdalene has sat alone on her porch thinking: either this is going to be the end or something is going to happen to stop this from being the end, and also waiting for the rain like everyone else, waiting outside on the porch because her house has no air conditioning and some of the windows are stuck shut.

Twice now over these weeks she had watched several thick gray clouds float across the sky like rafts moving in a still pool of water, briefly eclipsing the sun, threatening rain. Then they would move on or disappear, like today, the sun coming through the trees again, baking the ground into a cracked brown crust. Something has to happen, Magdalene thinks. Something.

Joe

Joe Wallace has been walking for two days now through these thick unforgiving woods, the tall narrow trees jutting out from the ground like crooked black fingers. The dead branches on the ground get caught around his ankles and feet as he walks. Yet he persists, slicing his way through the woods like a shiv. He doesnt know how exactly he ended up here, how it is that he is wandering with no food or drink, no real idea of where he is going now. But he knows this: he is in these woods, and he has to end up somewhere or he will die. And he does not want to die. He knows this too, feels it. It's in his gut.

Magdalene

Magdalene stretches her arms over her head and looks out at her yard. Except for the narrow clearing where a quartermilelong gravel driveway is cut, leading to the road that goes into town, the yard and her small house are surrounded by woods. There are several footpaths which her husband had cut last fall, just months before he left her, but these paths dont lead anywhere except into more woods and they are all mostly littered with dead branches and dying growth.

The cleared land around Magdalene's house is no more than two hundred feet in diameter and although she owns nearly twenty-two acres, she cannot clear any more of the land on her own, nor does she want to.

There is a tractor in the yard, but it is rusted and needs a new set of plugs. The weeds grow up through the tractor's undercarriage, past the axles, into the engine, where they further dry out and become cracked and split at the ends.

At the edge of the clearing is a rusty Chevy truck which Magdalene uses to drive into town for groceries. But she rarely leaves the property now that her husband is gone. There is also a horse that grazes around the yard, but there is nothing for the animal to eat now. Magdalene can see the horse's ribs, a row of pressured hoops, serried under its dry and dusty coat like an oddly-shaped birdcage cauled with flesh.

It is getting dark, the light now transient as ever, the yellow streaks of sun bleeding a deep orange then turning again until the streaks become violet, purple, then disappear as the sky grows black and starfilled, those stars a passel of myriad blank and unwinking eyes spread over a smooth dark scrim, clear and void of color: a black halcyon sea. Magdalene stands and flips on the porchlight. She walks inside and turns on all the lights in the house now.

Joe

Joe keeps walking. He uses the moonlight now to see where he is putting his feet and he thinks about deer as he walks. The shooting and eating of them. He remembers hunting with his father once. In woods much like these. Those far away gray dawns on which he could see his breath in front of him, his father's thick hand landing on his shoulder to alert him of a doe in the clearing, pressing hard into his collarbone as if to confirm the animal's existence. Joe is hungry now. Tired.

But time has collapsed into itself now so that it is like one long string that has been coiled around and around some endless spool and you cannot see the beginning or the end of it and you cannot tell exactly which part you are looking at, only that you are looking, but can make no guess at the string's length, where it ends and where it begins, or if it even does at all: like a fishing line pulled taut by something deep and unknowable in the bowels of some murky body of water.

Joe sees a light now that is not the moonlight he has been seeing for the past few hours. It is a yellow light, an unnatural light. Houselight, he thinks. He walks toward it, his figure a strange chiaroscuro moving faster down the dry and overgrown path, tripping on branches, falling almost, hurrying now.

Magdalene

The open expanse of woods, now dry and dark and cold, seems hungry and vacant, an infinite space that surrounds Magdalene's small house and bit of land, but also goes on to surround the little village of Sun Louisiana just a piece away from where Magdalene lives, its roads circuitously cutting their way from building to serried building, becoming a sort of maze: a crooked network of red clay and gravel or macadam strings which go from or between each nearly falling or fallen structure, and Magdalene, as she steps back out onto her now-lit porch, thinks she hears a noise coming from out there in that expanse, where all she can see now is the crooked black lines of pine upon pine jutting out from the ground, it seems, slashing the black sheet of sky which sits behind them so that these trees look like grotesque piano keys, or narrow, wind-tortured tombstones. It is very dark out now, but Magdalene can see something—or someone—out there. She watches.

Joe

Joe is standing at the edge of the woods now. He is looking across the dark clearing at the small lit house and he can see a person's silhouette on the front porch looking out, looking at him, it feels like. He doubts anyone can see him though. He can see a horse. He can hear it snorting and stomping its roughshod hooves against the hard and dusty ground. He can smell it, its warmth, and he can see its eye vaguely reflecting the moonlight, a black and brown globule set in its angular skull like a large ball bearing shot into a treetrunk.

Joe pushes aside a thin, almost leafless branch. What leaves it has are dry and brown and cracked. The leaves fall off onto the ground as Joe moves the branch out of his way. He walks into the moonlit clearing toward the small house. He walks toward the porchlight, shading his eyes as if he were looking into the sun.

Magdalene

Magdalene knows if she turns and runs, whoever this is coming up to the porch would just follow her in and do as they wish with her. She figures the best thing to do is stand her ground and wait for this figure to approach. Maybe they arent a bad person, she thinks. Maybe they just need some help. Everyone needs help, good folks and bad. If I can help this person, maybe they wont hurt me. Maybe I'll be okay.

Magdalene watches the figure approach the steps. It is shading its eyes from the mosquitosoaked porchlight, holding a hand over its brow as if in some strange salute.

Mam? the figure says tenuously.

I aint got money, Magdalene says. You best get.

That's not what I'm here for, mam.

Well, what then?

Food, mam. I havent ate in days.

Magdalene says: Well, I aint got much food. But you're welcome to what I do have, I suppose.

I appreciate it. By the way, I'm Joe. Then he says: Joe Wallace.

Magdalene looks at this man from where she stands on her porch. He's smaller than she first realized. His hair is brown and long in the front, just covering his eyebrows. The rest is cut close to his head. He's about her age, she figures.

I'm Magdalene. Come up then. And mind those mosquitoes, less you want to get bit.

Magdalene takes this Joe Wallace for country folk, like herself, by his short way of speaking to her, and she has always trusted country folk, unless they're up to no good, which she could see in their eyes, mostly, and this Joe Wallace hasnt the look of no good in his eyes.

Magdalene steps aside, and Joe walks up the steps. He stands directly in front of her now, looking into her face. Her eyes.

Joe

Joe thinks he knows where he is now, knows where he has come from, why he has been walking and where he is trying to get to: and this is good. But he cannot tell this woman about it yet. He looks at Magdalene as if he'd known her for a very long time. Her hair is long and brown, almost to her waist, and she does not have it pulled back like a housewife would, but it is wavy and mellifluous, caressing her shoulders and falling down her back and arms. Joe is standing there in the mosquito swarm, looking at her.

Well, come in then, Magdalene says. Like I said, I got a little bit of food inside you can eat.

They walk into the house and into the kitchen. Magdalene stands in front of the refrigerator. Her hand is on the unopened door. She looks at Joe, who is watching her. And he knows that he will not die now, at least not for a long time, as long as he is standing here in this light like this, his heartmuscles pushing the blood through his body into each pulsing part of him.

He looks at her. Takes in her image like he would a breath, wanting to ask her something, but not knowing how to make his question into words, how to string all these pieces of sound together to make something whole, something that she would understand and would think is good. So he stands tacitly under the warm kitchen light, trying to paste each word together in his head so that they are all in their right place before he says them.

Joe steps forward a little, toward Magdalene. Her hand is still on the refrigerator door, not moving, yet pulsing. He can see that. Her pulse. He puts his hand out, touches Magdalene's arm. Then he opens his mouth:

Tell me one thing, he says. Can you just tell me one thing?

Magdalene

Yes? she asks, letting Joe's hand move slowly up and down and across her arm, still feeling it there after he removes it, like some phantom limb, not believing this is happening to her now. Yes? It's a question, but what Magdalene is thinking and has been since Joe first walked into her yard and then touched her and even after he let her go is yes, the thought itself feeling like a breath of air being pushed from her lungs and through her mouth and into the room for Joe to breathe in himself now. Yes. Something has happened now.

She stands and waits for Joe's question, to which she already has her answer prepared.

December 21 1987

Vermena

Let me tell you about Joe Wallace. He come up here one day lookin for work. I told him he was gonna have to wait till Mr Bivens, my husband, got back, bein I dont make them decisions. Mr Bivens wouldnt be back till late the next day anyway, I tole him. Tole him he went to trade with Peaches Covington's old man Fox over in Opelousas. Most folks'd think I was crazy for tellin this old stranger that I was up in the house by myself without my husband around, but I aint scared a no skinny little boys such as Joe Wallace. I know where he come from. I knew his daddy. Besides, my sons was around the place. My old man wouldnt leave me to tend to all this land by myself. I couldnt even if I wanted to. Got my bad back to worry with.

Anyway this Joe he just ast me for work, so I told him to come back tomorrow evenin or better, the next day after that, and he said thank you and then he asked me where he could get somethin to eat, that he was dyin of hunger. I just told him sorry, I couldnt help, that the drought was killin us just like it was everyone else, and I couldnt do nothin to help him as far as food was concerned.

We was as poor as the next person and couldnt hardly afford to feed ourselves let alone somebody else. A criminal besides.

Say, I said to him, what you doin around here anyway? I thought you was up in Angola for that murder some years back.

He said he had been, but that he werent anymore. That they let him out. Hm, I thinks, a convicted murderer out in the streets again. Well, I didnt much care neither way and told him to get on, that he could come back the next day if he wanted, and that was the last I seen of him for a while. He never did come back. Truth be told, I didnt really care what happened to him. I ast my husband when he got back from Opelousas if Joe Wallace come around again and he said he aint heard nothin from him, so we both just figured him gone on. Off to somewheres else. We didnt spend much time thinkin about it. We had bigger fishes to fry up what with that damn drought and all. It wasnt until Miss Tucker come into Shorty's one day lookin for some plugs for that tractor her old deadbeat husband left behind, and Shorty he ast her what she knew about puttin plugs in a old tractor and she tole him that she didnt know nothin about it, but that someone was out over on her place and was gonna fix the thing for her. Then's when we all knew where old Wallace had landed hisself. We just knew it. Shorty he never even made the connection until after, so, needless to say, he didnt tell her about Wallace and his conviction and to maybe watch out for him, especially since she be out there in them woods all alone and everything, but you know Shorty, he a little on the slow side sometimes. And like I said, we had bigger fishes to fry up, so aint no one bothered to go out there and tell Miss Tucker the truth about the boy until it was already too late.

You see the reason she didnt know about that awful murder was because she moved out here to Sun from Poplarville Mississippi a good deal after the crime done happened, and folks had plumb stopped talkin about it by then. She had moved here with that deadbeat husband of hers since he owned him a piece a land outside of town and since he had him some notions that he was gonna farm it, raise cattle on it, make a decent living. They stayed out there and he didnt do much of anything cept pile up some debt and put a gallon a Old Crow in hisself about once every week.

True he had that little house there, a little circle of cleared land around it that he done cleared hisself. Had him a horse, a truck, that tractor. But he just seemed to up and quit on Miss Tucker after a while. Walkin in to town every day and runnin up tabs at The Horse, fallin off the barstool and sleepin on the sidewalk sometimes. That Tuck used to be a prizefighter. That's the shame of the whole thing. He used to make him a pretty decent livin before he took to drinkin so much when they moved out here.

Then this little tramp come up from New Orleans lookin for work at The Horse, started tendin bar there—Ray, the owner, figured it'd bring in more customers if he had him a pretty woman behind the bar—and she starts tanglin up with Tuck, Miss Tucker's deadbeat husband. Next thing we know, them two ups and takes off back to New Orleans, leavin Miss Tucker by herself with all that land to tend to. And funny thing was, she would never mention it to any of us when she come into town for groceries and whatnot. She'd just smile and wave same as before, and believe me, we'd be dyin to ask her for all the details but figured it wouldnt be very Christian of us to do so, so we didnt never.

Then the drought came. Back in April I think it started.

And then Joe Wallace he come up to my place lookin for work late August or thereabouts, then a couple days later Shorty said Miss Tucker had been in for some plugs and said she had someone out on the place who was gonna put em in for her. That's when we all knew. But like I said with the drought and all bein as bad as it was, no one really took the time to ride out there at first and tell her who this Joe Wallace really was. Lookin back, it probably would've been the Christian thing of us to do. But what is it they say about hindsight? It's always a hunderd percent? Somethin like that anyway.

August 28 1987

Magdalene's house is small. The paint on the outside is cracked and peeling—the swelling sun bakes it as hard and dry as it does the earth. If the house were alive it would be dying the same slow death as the ground on which it is built. But it is not alive. It is small and made of wood and nails and tin and glass.

The house is square. What paint is left on it is white and peeling off in shards. Its roof is a rusted sheet of tin with a three inch overhang, hardly enough to stand under in the rain. The windows— there are eight of them, two on each wall—are each framed with a dark green sill, the green peeling into thin shreds like the rest of the paint on the house.

The porch in front of the house is slatted with rotting two by fours, and there are some missing. Like someone's teeth that have started to rot away, their mouth a broken accordion. There are two rocking chairs and a swing on the porch. The swing hangs from two rusty chains and it hangs low. Close to the rotting slats. Like a waterlogged hammock. Even a child's feet would scrape at the boards if he were to swing there.

Magdalene

She doesnt want to get up, feels she cant get up now, knowing that he's in there somewhere, sleeping or maybe even awake already, before her. They'd been up most of the night, talking, her and Joe, so it's possible he is still asleep. She'd fixed him a pallet on the floor in the den. She hopes he was comfortable there. He said he'd be fine, especially after trudging around and sleeping in those woods for the past few days. She hadnt asked him why he had been doing that or where he was coming from, but she would. Soon. She would have to if he was going to stay out here with her like this.

But right now she's worrying he is already up. She's not used to having a man in her house anymore. A stranger besides.

Magdalene listens. It's quiet. Had she dreamed all of this? Is Joe Wallace someone she imagined? She doesnt think so. She looks at her arm where he had touched her. She rubs her hands over it, looks up at the ceiling, then rolls over and puts her face in her pillow.

Joe

Joe is up already. He is looking out the living room window at the tractor in the yard. He is wondering if it runs, if he could use the Bushhog that's on the ground behind it to cut some of these dead weeds in Magdalene's yard. He wants to help. It's the least he could do, he figures. The machine looks to be in bad shape though. All that dead grass around it. But Joe knows that most tractors will fire up no matter how long they sit there, as long as they have fuel in them. When Magdalene gets up, he'll have to ask her about it. That is, if she doesnt mind him staying for a while.

Joe walks out to the porch, stretches his arms, looking at the yard, horse, tractor, and the truck. Everything has the weight of death upon it. But Joe keeps thinking about that tractor, if he could get it running. He walks into the yard, kicking up a cloud of dust under his boots. He stops in front of the gaunt horse, rubs his hand over its snout, runs his fingers through its mane. He looks around for a hose so he could water the animal down, but doesnt see one, and he decides to ask Magdalene if she has one in back of the house. That is, if the well hasnt dried up yet.

Joe walks over to the tractor and sits in its chair. He pulls out the choke and sets the throttle. The key is in the ignition, so he turns it. Nothing. He pushes in the clutch, puts it in NEUTRAL, then tries again. Still nothing. Joe gets out of the chair, moves to the side of the machine, lifts up the hood and looks at the engine. He sees the weeds coming up through the tractor's workings. He pulls at some of the weeds. Then he checks the oil. Fine. He walks around to the back and he unscrews the gas cap, looks in the tank. He cant see anything so he pushes the tractor back and forth a bit on its large tires and he listens for the slosh of fuel in the tank. It sounds about half full. Then he walks back around to the front of the tractor and he stands on the wheel. He pulls back the hood and looks at the engine. Then he pulls out one of the plugs, wipes it off with his shirt. Joe scrapes the dirt off the end of one of them with his fingernail, sees that the porcelain insulator is cracked and blistered and the points are burned and that the thing couldnt possibly be firing like this so he removes the others which look about the same and then he decides that all the tractor needs is a new set of plugs and it'd likely run decent enough.

When Magdalene wakes up, Joe is going to ask her three things: if her well is dried up, and if it isnt, if she's got a garden hose in back of the house so he can water the horse down, and if she can run into town and get some plugs for the tractor. He might also ask her a fourth one, depending on her response to those: if she doesnt mind him staying around the place for a while to help out, being that she's out here by herself. Since she's been so kind to feed him, he figures it's the least he can do to return the favor. He is going to wait for Magdalene to wake up so he can ask her these things. He decides to wait on the porch, in her chair.

Magdalene

She finally lifts her head from the pillow when she hears what sounds like someone walking on her porch, the creaking and groaning sound of old and weathered wood an unmistakable sound, especially to Magdalene, who has grown accustomed to this noise, has come to almost rely on it over the years, taking it as a sign that her husband was finally home from town. When she used to hear this, she would roll over in bed and pretend to sleep. She could finally sleep when he was home. Sometimes he would come into the room and just pass out next to her. Others he would shake her until she turned to him, saw his naked body standing there. Then he would climb onto her groaning into her ear the whole time: the bed creaking now, the metal legs scratching at the wood floor. Leaving tight and ugly grooves. Then he would stop groaning, stay on top of her for a minute, then finally roll over and sleep. Heavy. The next morning she'd watch him from the kitchen window pull out of the yard, turn onto the driveway, and lurch his truck over the clay potholes which he had promised and promised to fill but never did.

Magdalene walks out of her room and into the bathroom across the hall. She turns on the light and closes the door behind her. She looks at herself in the mirror, turns on the tap and washes out her eyes. The pressure has gone down considerably recently, but Magdalene is still hopeful: she figures that it must rain any day now. That the earth will again be soaked, the rainwater trickling down to her thirsty well lying under the dirt and loam and clay and rock.

When she finishes in the bathroom Magdalene walks into the kitchen and plugs in the percolator and starts the coffee.

Joe

Joe hasnt smelled coffee in weeks. The smell is so strong he can almost see it in the air on the porch where he sits rocking in Magdalene's chair. He rocks back and takes in a deep breath, looks out at the horse in the yard again. It snorts at the ground, blowing up little clouds of dust and dead yellowing grass. Then he hears the screen door open behind him. He turns around. He is facing Magdalene now who is standing in the threshold. The door slaps against the frame behind her. She jumps.

September 1 1987

Tuck

A whore. And here I am mixing up with her and done left my wife for her and moved to this city with all its trash and all its sad and crazy people for her. This whore who I know would stab me through the back in a second before I could even turn around to catch the gleam of the knifeblade in her skinny and quivering and drunken hand. And I still cant figure for the life of me why I done this, why I'm still laying next to her.

I turn over and put my hand under my cheekbone to prop up my head so I can look at Mae. She's sleeping and her mouth is open and she's breathing in little puffs of air, then pushing them out through her nostrils. The bedsheet is draped over her thigh, and the rest of her body seems to sprout from under it, her soft lines and the cave of her belly: it all disgusts me now.

But when I first seen her behind the bar at The Horse I knew I was in for it. She had on these jeans that would make a soul weep, make you forget your name: they hugged the curves of her just so.

When I first walked in the bar and seen her, she was twisting the cap off a beer bottle and she must've twisted too hard, must've been holding the bottle too tight and in just the right place because as she was twisting, her arms pulled taut and squeezing against her, the bottle broke at the neck and she dropped it, the jagged pieces hitting the cement floor and the blood already coming from her hand and sliding down her arm and her face just in shock.

No one was really paying any attention to her and couldnt hear the glass breaking, what with the music and all, but I seen it, must've been the only one, and I walked in and behind the bar and grabbed a rag from the sink and wrapped it around her wet and bleeding and shaking hand and she looked up at me with these soft eyes and said thank you. I didnt say anything, just looked at her face, eyes, down at the white dishrag that I had tied around her hand and its ends hanging down like pigtails, a red blossom coming up where the cut was.

It's my first day, she said. What shit luck I got.

I still didnt say anything. Just looked at her hair coming down over her shoulders. I couldnt keep my eyes off her.

What are the chances? she said.

I shrugged. You okay?

I'll be fine. Thanks for helping.

She bent down to clean up the glass and I watched the lines of her back as they curved. People were starting to look now. Or maybe they had been the whole time. I hadnt even noticed.

It got so I was going to The Horse every damned day after that. Drinking too much, running up a tab I knew I wouldnt pay, talking to this girl behind the bar and trying not to think about my wife back home. It got so that when I was at home, all I could think about was this girl at the bar and I couldnt hardly even look my wife in her eyes anymore. It was awful. Plumb awful.

I'd come home drunk and wanting to screw something, so I'd do it to my wife but all I could think of was this girl at the bar. I'd keep my eyes open so I'd have to see my wife under me, but I'd see the girl's face looking back up at me instead. So I'd close my eyes and I'd still see that girl under me. She was everywhere. Even on the backs of my eyelids.

I started hating my wife. The idea of her anyways. I spent more time talking to this girl, less time with my wife. The guilt was the only bad part. And it got worse. It got to where the guilt was so terrible, I had to leave home and try to disappear for good. It was all I could do.

The night I decided to leave, we were lying in bed at Mae's trailer, and Mae was smoking a cigarette.

Let's leave, I said.

To where?

I was thinking of the city.

She said: New Orleans?

Yeah, why not? There's plenty of bars there. We could find work easy.

I know, I lived there, remember? But what would you do?

Hell, I could tend bar too, I said. I spend enough time there as it is.

When you want to leave? she said.

Why not now? Tonight?

Okay, she said, let me get my things.

It was just like that. So we left.

The city was hot and the streets were sticky and crammed with drunks and biblethumpers. They were all mixed together, like a pot of gumbo. Nights were the worst. The humidity was enough to kill you. We'd walk the streets, me and Mae, and we looked for work in any bar we could find.

Then Mae got work at a strip joint on Bourbon Street serving drinks. They promised her she wouldnt have to dance or take off her clothes, and she told me she wouldnt do that anyways, no matter how good the money was and no matter how much we needed it.

I got work as a dishwasher and a cook in a little restaurant on Decatur Street and we fixed it to where we both got off work at the same time. It only took me about ten minutes to walk from my job to Mae's so after I got done I'd walk to get her and then we'd walk down Bourbon past all the bars until we got to our second floor apartment off Esplanade, away from most of the noise.

Things were going good for the first few weeks. My wife wasnt trying to find me, me and Mae made enough money to pay the rent, and drinks were mostly free for both of us where she was working.

Early mornings we'd sit on our balcony and watch the sun come up and watch the streets steam as the streetsweepers slid past pushing the litter from the night before into the neutral grounds where folks were already jogging or walking their dogs. They were just getting up, about to start their days, me and Mae was just ending ours. It was a backwards way of life, but it was fun at the time and we kind of liked things that way.

We'd usually go in around five and have one last drink before we took off our clothes and went to bed. Her body was so new to me. I couldnt keep my hands off it. And she was happy to let me do whatever I wanted. Sometimes we'd screw until we couldnt hardly see straight. Those were the good times. But they didnt last.

We'd been in the city since late April. By midsummer, things were starting to get bad. I stopped meeting Mae at work and I'd just go to some bar by myself and drink until I couldnt hardly stand up anymore. Then I'd walk home and fall into bed. Sometimes Mae would be there, sometimes she wouldnt. We got to where we started living our own lives.

I started feeling guilty about things turning sour so I decided one night after work to drop by Mae's job and have a drink with her and then walk home with her like we used to. I walked into the bar and there was Mae up on the pole running a creamy leg up its side.

And everyone was staring at her too.

I sat down at the bar and ordered a drink and watched Mae dance and take off her clothes. In front of all those eyes. And it was then I knew she had been screwing some of these men too. I just knew it. That she was a whore. And that she had screwed me just the same.

The fights started, then got worse. We'd throw bottles at each other, tip furniture over, broke a window once.

Some nights are okay. We get home in the morning, drink, screw each other, then sleep. We still have money to live off of. More than enough now that Mae's taking off her clothes. But when I look at her now all I can think is: whore. I think about my wife and how she wasnt a whore and how I'm lying in bed with one now. The guilt sets in good then. It gets so that I cant hardly look at Mae. And that's when I start thinking about home. And my wife. And I wonder what this time without me has done to her, if it's turned her into a whore too. But I know that it hasnt. She was a real good woman. Magdalene. I miss her.

I roll over again, away from Mae. It's September now, and hot still. I lie on my back and stare up at the ceiling, pull the sheets off my chest. The fan's spinning fast overhead and I try to follow one of the blades with my eyes by rolling them around in my head. Then I get dizzy. Nauseous. And just like that I decide it's time to leave Mae and go back home. Back to my wife. I'll be out of here in two days.

December 21 1987

Vermena

My back been givin me trouble ever since I had Darryl—you know the one we calls Outlaw. It was one of them breech births, when the baby come out all sideways or backways and enough to damn near tear your insides out or tear you in half if nothin else. I had him at home since he was my first boy and I didnt know no better at the time and the doctor he couldnt get out to the place anyways since all the rain we was havin that summer—not a thing like it was a few months ago back in August when Joe Wallace showed up and all that trouble started with Miss Tucker and her old man. Even Pastor Varner got involved too if you can believe that.

Anyways I was in so much pain and screamin for someone to kill me, please kill me, and we knew aint no doctor gonna get there in time to help deliver this baby and that I was gonna die if that child wasnt pulled out. So Mr Bivens, my husband, he had to eventually just yank little Darryl from my body. And Lord how the blood did come out of me. So much that I felt like I had been completely emptied and my head got all light and tingly and my whole body felt like it was a feather and I was floatin right up to Heaven. I swear I could even see myself floatin upways into the sky and the real part of me down on the bed with Mr Bivens standing beside me with that little purple baby in his hands and holdin him up just so like he was inspectin a carburetor and the blood and the afterbirth just drippin off that baby like oil, all thick and oozy and black-lookin. And here I was, all bloodless and light-feelin, and seein two of me at once, one heavenward and the other earthbound, bedbound, and all I could think about was that little boy, that umbilical tube hangin from his stomach and slappin against Mr Bivens's forearm like a tail, and wonderin if that boy was gonna make it. Since I couldnt hear nothin from wherever the part of me was that was watchin all this, I couldnt tell if that boy was cryin or not, and since he was all purple in color, I kind afeared he wasnt breathin, that maybe Mr Bivens needed to smack him on the back good to sort of jumpstart him. And just as soon as I thought this, as if he could hear me thinkin it, Mr Bivens up and slapped that boy on the bottom with the heel of his hand and then that baby went to screamin and hollerin on (or at least, his mouth was movin so—I couldnt hear nothin, like I said), so it was then that I knew he was breathin and that he was gonna be all right. But since I was somewheres outside of my body and I could feel myself floatin up higher and higher, I was worried that I wasnt gonna be all right so I started lookin upward to where part of me seemed to be goin and I started talkin to Jesus, to God, to whoever was listenin and I started pleadin with them to let me stay here on earth with my new baby and Mr Bivens so I could take care of them proper, like I was intended to. And someone musta been listenin that day, I tell you, cause next thing I knew I could hear that baby cryin and Mr Bivens callin to me—Vermena, Vermena, Vermena—but all this soundin like I was hearin it through the end of a big culvert but like I was bein pushed through it so that the sound was louder and louder and closer and closer and very next thing I know, I'm lookin out through my own eyes and I feel this bright pain all down my back and my front and my insides too and I hear Mr Bivens sayin, Thank you, Jesus, oh thank you thank you. Then: Vermena is you okay baby? Then: God I love you woman. Then he handed me the little one so I could take care of him. But the bottom line is it was that damned breech birth that started me up with all these back problems I got. And they aint got better. In fact they got worse over the years. And that was just another reason why I wasnt so anxious about goin out to Miss Tucker's place to tell her the truth about Joe Wallace.

Also like I was sayin earlier about us not warnin her and it not bein the Christian thing of us to do, you have to understand that we had a lot on our minds what with the drought and all. We needed a good rain to get the crops goin and keep our horses and cattle alive. But after Shorty told us about Miss Tucker comin in and askin about plugs for that tractor of hers and we all fount out that Joe Wallace was stayin on her place, we all just sort of mulled over the whole thing for a day or two. I had told Mr Bivens to go down there and have him a talk with Miss Tucker and Joe, but he got tied up around here and didnt. And then nobody heard nothin at all, not for a few days anyway, and we just sort a put it all up on the back burner, like I said. Besides, none of us had no idea that Miss Tucker's damn husband would come back lookin for her to forgive him for runnin off with that little whore from the bar, that he'd be lookin to kill that young boy Joe Wallace as if the whole mess was his fault. Hell by the time Tuck done got the mind to come home, it was late into August or early September and hadnt rained in damn near five months. So did Tuck have the right to do what he done, specially since he been gone for more than four months his own self with some whore he met in a bar? Well I dont rightly know. I aint one to be meddlin in the business a other folks any old way. I got my own life to tend to.

September 2 1987

Magdalene's horse is dying. It drops its gaunt and moribund body onto the dirt and begins to breathe erratic puffs of air from its nose. Little mushrooms of dust and grass cloud around its snout, its worried black eyes. The animal knows it is dying, the way animals always know these things.

The muscles on the horse's neck and side and pasterns twitch. Its withers and hindquarters are blacksoaked with sweat. The horse flashes its tail at the ground when a fly or a mosquito lands on it, but is otherwise still. A whiteyellow foam is coagulating around the animal's mouth and the green crust in its eyes is so it can hardly open them now.

The dust on the horse's brindled coat turns to mud as it mixes with the animal's sweat, creating streaks, lines, cracks and patterns that resemble some recondite manmade design, as if the animal's body is now the wall of some ancient cave over which scores of ontological myths and stories, all esoteric now, have been etched out in boar's blood and hieroglyphs. Attempting to limn the beginning of things. And the end of them too.

Magdalene

Death hangs in the air now and Magdalene can almost feel its nonpulse as it settles down on her horse, who she cannot feed nor water nor comfort now. Joe watches this too but Magdalene knows he is as helpless to stop this as she.

Joe sits forward in his rocking chair. The porchslats creak under the weight of him.

We should put her down, he says. She's suffering.

Magdalene turns her face to Joe's. She says: I cant. Not yet at least.

We cant feed her. She's dying. I cant watch this.

Well dont, Magdalene tells him. We're dying too, you know, she says.

Dont say that.

But we are.

But now Joe is quiet. It looks to Magdalene as if he is in another world now.

Joe

Joe is thinking again about prison. He looks over at Magdalene but he cannot bring himself to tell her about it yet. He thinks about Saint Louis, and the dead body, shot through the head, and the missing girl who turned up near Independence off the interstate hysterical and screaming about her father being killed and her being taken, kidnapped, and the men who did it, but she couldnt say for sure who they were or what they looked like and she wouldnt testify and finally just disappeared and no one heard from her again and it was Joe Wallace who had been picking up a truckload of clay and sod from some fellow Thompson just north of Saint Louis and driving straight down 55 into Louisiana and stopping for gas in Independence when the girl showed up and everything just seemed too convenient and he was arrested and blamed for a string of robberies and a murder and a kidnapping too. Although he was convicted only on the charge of kidnapping.

Joe Wallace who was put to jail at nineteen years old, an honest boy.

He was released twelve years later and he used his small

stipend to ride a Greyhound bus from the Louisiana State Penitentiary in Angola to as far as it would take him to Bogalusa and then walking from there to Sun, his hometown, his birthplace, where everyone knew him—all the oldtimers at least, since his immediate family had moved from there after his conviction—where he hoped someone would take sympathy on him and give him work, a place to stay. But no one would. There was an awful drought that was killing the town from the inside out, so he had found himself languishing in the woods, sleeping among the pines and the deer which he had no gun to shoot and so he had not eaten for days.

Then he had stumbled into a clearing and had met a woman and things had started to change for him. But he could not forgive God or whoever was responsible for his years in jail, his rejection by his family, his people, his utter loss of time.

But now he must think of some way to tell Magdalene of all this: about his years in prison, what he saw there. He must tell her before she finds out some other way. If he doesnt, she will never trust him and she will likely make him leave. And Joe cant let this happen because he thinks he loves her now.

July 17 1975

Travis

Travis was already up making too much noise, blasting the news on TV, knocking things over. His friend Doyle slept through most of this, but finally he woke up.

Travis was standing over him. Get up, he said.

He was nudging Doyle's back with the toe of his boot: a steel-tipped, turquoise-dyed-snakeskin atrocity with clanky pewter spurs nailed to the heels.

Get up. He kicked him again. Hard in the small of his back.

Doyle rolled over. He looked up. Travis was already dressed, hair slicked back black and shining, cigarettes rolled up into the sleeve of his small white T-shirt. He was gnawing on a toothpick, damp little splinters of wood floating down like dandruff onto Doyle and his makeshift pallet that was made out of a dirty sleepingbag and a large yellow blanket.

What the hell you so cranked about? Doyle said, his eyes still halfshut with sleep.

We gotta split man, Travis spat. Cops are on us again.

Doyle stood and put his fists into the small of his back,

stretched, and began walking around the tiny motel room, looking for his things. Travis handed him a cigarette.

Thanks, Doyle said. He sat down to put his boots on.

Within five minutes Doyle was ready and Travis was closing the door behind them. It was warm outside although the sun was barely out yet. A thin fog hung lazily close to the asphalt lot.

After the men had tossed their bags into the trunk, Travis walked across the parking lot to the small office to return the key to their room. The oriental man at the desk was drinking coffee and reading a newspaper.

Anything good? Travis said. He tossed the key onto the counter and waited for some look of recognition from the man. After seeing none, he said: Say you know about how far Texas is from here Pops?

Let's see, Saint Louis about a hour and it probably take twelve more to get to Dallas. I not really sure though.

Twelve, Travis said to himself thinking. And then looking around to make sure the room was empty, he reached into the back of his pants and pulled out a stolen Colt Single Action .32-20 Army Revolver and pointed it at the man behind the desk and said: Now how about emptying out that there register for me chief?

I'm sorry? the man said.

You heard me, Travis said. I think you heard me fine old man.

The man paused then, opened the drawer and handed Travis what was inside. His hands were shaking.

Travis took the money. He said: You're a good man.

Then he began to lower his gun. He was walking backwards out of the office when someone, a girl, came out of the bathroom, saying: Daddy, the faucet on that sink still not working right. I th— The girl turned and looked at Travis, who now held the gun on her, smiling at her too as if he had just won the lottery.

Well, hello there, he said, looking her up and down, keeping the gun on her. She was beautiful, looked to be about eighteen, silky black hair falling to her waist, long tan legs growing from a pair of tiny white shorts.

What's your name? he said.

The girl looked at her father. Her eyes had widened into half dollars. Daddy? was all she could manage. She let out a short scream that sounded more like a hiccup, fell to her knees and sobbed sporadically.

You leave her alone, the man said. I give you the money already. Now you go.

Travis smiled a salesman's grin. Now, now, chief. Dont get all snippy. I'm just tryin to be polite.

He turned to the girl. Stand up honey. Come on, stand up. Then he pointed the gun at the wall behind the desk and shot. A picture that was hanging there fell and broke against the floor.

The girl screamed again, then stood with her hands cupped over her ears to muffle the blast. She was sobbing heavily now.

Good, Travis said. Now how about coming over here?

Then the man spoke up: I said to leave her alone. He was now inching forward. But Travis turned and pointed the Colt at him again, squeezing the trigger now two times: two white flashes lighting up the dusty room. The two bullets went into the man's forehead and tore through his skull, their soft lead points flattening into mushrooms on their way out, the force of them pushing the man's body into the wall behind him. His head hit the wainscoting and he slid down to the floor, tracing a paint-roller-sized smear of blood and brainmatter and cordite along the wall as he went down.

The girl breathed in hard, as if her throat were closing up on her. She ran to her father and fell over his body, sobbing into his shirt, trying to breathe. Travis took advantage of this time to look around the room for anything worth taking. Then Doyle came in. Frantic.

What in hell are you doing? Jesus Christ. *Oh Jesuschrist.*

Doyle ran back outside and climbed into the car. Travis heard him start the engine and saw Doyle's arm shifting it into gear. The car lurched forward. Then stopped. Travis waited. He knew Doyle would not leave without him.

Doyle

The first time Doyle got scared of Travis was when they were thirteen and living next door to each another in Waveland Mississippi. The boys had been working on a treehouse in Travis's backyard, collecting wood from around their neighborhood, at the beach, or from other kids' treehouses, and bringing it back to Travis's as their own. They would haul their plunder like two marauders to the base of the tree they had selected and then they would pile the wood on the ground.

After working two afternoons the boys had finished it and were sitting high into the woods drinking Cokes and looking down at how small everything was.

One day Travis said: You dare me to jump? He spit a stream of Coke from his mouth, watching it arc down to the ground like water spraying from a fountainhead, counting the seconds it took to get there.

Doyle laughed. He knew a jump from this height was enough to break your legs or kill you even.

But Travis was standing now. He really was going to jump.

Are you crazy? If you do that, you'll break your ass.

Travis looked down again, then drank from his Coke and spit another brown stream of it to the ground. This time he counted almost three seconds—one Mississippi, two Mississippi, three Mississ—before it splattered onto the dirt.

Doyle stood. He put his hand on Travis's shoulder.

Travis looked at him. He threw the glass bottle out of the treehouse and jumped after it, not even waiting for the glass to crash against the dirt. Doyle heard his friend hit the ground with a sound that reminded him of someone punching a horse in its side.

Then silence.

Doyle was afraid to look down, imagining a scene far worse than any story he had ever heard from his father about farming accidents or car crashes or the battles he had fought overseas. The men who had lost their body parts. The men who had died.

Holy hell, man, did you see that? Travis was yelling up at Doyle, his shirt covered with leaves, dirt, small twigs.

Doyle looked down. Travis was trying to stand, brushing the dirt from his clothes, unaware that his right leg was hanging like a snapped branch from his quivering body.

Travis, Jesus Christ. Your leg, Doyle said, his voice cracking into a near-inaudible pitch. As if he had blown into a dogwhistle.

Then Travis looked down, saw his leg dangling—broken—his jeans turning dark red, then black, where the bone had torn through his flesh, then his jeans, and was beginning to drip onto the leaves and dirt and his shoes. Travis fell out cold like some aging prizefighter who had finally taken his last blow to the head, the soft braintissue colliding with the unforgiving wall of skull surrounding it for the absolute and final time.

When Travis was released from the hospital two days later, his father made him and Doyle—after he had beaten them both—get rid of their treehouse. Travis couldnt climb the ladder to help dismantle the thing, so the boys had to build a fire around the base of the tree in which the treehouse was built.

They were to burn it down, Travis's father had said. Then he made them watch the hungry flames as they blackened their way up the side of the tree, growing and growing, turning from blue to white to yellow to orange, breathing as if a living thing, until those flames reached high enough to devour their work as well as God's completely.

Doyle is idling their stolen 1970 Chevy Malibu in front of the motel's office now. He cant make himself leave, so he puts it back into PARK to wait for Travis. Then he gets out and walks inside. He stops in the doorjamb and looks down.

Travis

Travis was on the floor, his knee pressed into a beautiful young girl's lowerback. He was holding her hands together and tying them at the wrists with a length of phonecord.

What the hell are you doing?

Just taking a little souvenir, Travis said. Can you give me a hand?

Doyle shook his head and turned to walk out of the place.

But Travis stood, pointing the gun at him. I think you should stay, he said.

Doyle raised his hands. His palms were facing out toward Travis. He held them there.

Travis bent back down to his work, then after a couple of minutes, he said: All right. Come help me put her in the backseat.

Doyle didnt say anything. He moved woodenly.

He helped shove the girl into the car, then Travis shut the door and they both walked to the back of the still-idling Chevrolet. Then they seemed to wait for something else to happen.

They drove. For an entire day and into the night they drove from Saint Louis and into Louisiana instead of Texas, keeping to Interstate 55 the whole way. A straight shot. By the time they saw the sign telling them they were within an hour and a half from New Orleans, Travis decided that he had enough of this girl and that he should drop her off somewhere so he could be free of her.

They pulled off into Independence about two hours north of New Orleans and Travis pushed the girl from the car. Then they drove south into the city where they would remain quietly and without circumstance for the next twelve years.

December 21 1987

Vermena

Truth is we dont know if Joe Wallace really done it or not. The murder I'm talkin about. We just assumed he did, since all the facts seemed to add up against him. Joe Wallace was one of these drifter types. Cept he didnt really drift nowheres but here around town. He was just strange acting most of the time. Too quiet. Sometimes he'd get him some work that'd bring him to other parts, but mostly he just stayed around here, workin on and off at the paper mill, pickin up odd jobs on folks' places, cleanin and fixin up and whatnot. But like I say: every now and again he'd get him some work that'd take him elsewhere, and that's what happened how come he got convicted of that murder and kidnappin. Or how come he actually done it, and thought he could get away with it at least.

He had gotten him some work over at this little nursery movin plants and uprootin hedges and waterin and fertilizin—you know, just general everyday work. The kind of work folks around here do. Well after about a week or two, his boss, Mr Mizell, he tole Joe Wallace that he needed to pick up a big load of some kind of sod and clay that he done ordered for this landscapin contract that he had out in Franklinton. But this special kind of sod he wanted was all the way up past Saint Louis. In Missouri. Quite a good piece from here. And Mizell couldnt leave his family for the week it'd take him to make the trip, so he ast Joe to do it. Said he'd lend him the truck and everything. Well Joe he was more than glad to take Mizell up on the offer, bein that he never been that far away from Louisiana before and since he loved wanderin and meanderin around any old way.

So he took the truck and he drove on up there by hisself.

He was gone bout three days, then he come back by way of fiftyfive and he stopped off in Independence. He had said in court it was cause he wanted to get him a bite to eat, gas up the truck, clean it off and whatnot. Well, that's when this little girl show up screamin about how she been kidnapped and raped and her daddy was dead and when they ast her where she was from she said near Saint Louis and here she was in Independence just at the same time as Joe Wallace was. Everybody thought it was just too damned much of a coincidence since several folks would later testify that they seen Joe wanderin around that gas station where the little girl turned up and that he had been in that parking lot for a good hour or so before leavin. So that's when they picked Joe up at his mama's house here in Sun and they brought him in.

Of course he denied the whole business. Said he didnt know nothin about no murders or kidnappings. But it just seemed too plain to everyone that he done it, so they convicted him right fast. Since the girl done left—we guessed her remaining family come down and got her (she said she didnt want to stay here to testify anyway, was too traumatized), them lawyers had to make them a pretty solid case with what they had, which I have to say wasnt much: but still they made the conviction. And that's just how we do things down here. Our courts and our justice system work right fast and we dont tolerate any wrongdoing and we dont waste a whole lot of time thinkin over things too much. We just put evil in its place. The devil where he belongs. A few folks around here get together and say you done something, then you done it and there aint much can be done to prove otherwise. That's exactly what happened with Joe Wallace.

So even though they was only able to get him for the lesser charge of kidnapping, not murder and rape too, what with that girl not here to testify and not wantin to be mixed up in all this, I assume, off he went to Angola, like we had all been hopin for too. But he was out in just twelve years and knockin on my door lookin for work and then shackin up with Miss Tucker the next day it seemed. Hm. Should've fried him if you ask me. But like I say, and I say again, I dont like to go meddlin around in other folks's business nohow. I just stick to myself mainly. Fact is we all do around here. That's how come places like Sun be such nice ones to live.

September 2 1987

The village of Sun Louisiana is flanked on the west by Enon, on the north by Bogalusa and on the east by Mississippi. Where Highway 21 intersects with Highway 16, leading into the village, a long embankment slopes down toward the Bogue Chitto River, which is shaded by tall and heaving pines, their long thin shadows like a row of sentinels watching over the white sandshores and the translucent goldbrown water, through which fat and lethargic catfish, graybrown and silt-covered, languish at the cool riverbottom.

Also where these highways intersect is Shorty's—a convenience store where you can buy anything from baitworms to chocolate milk, lawnmower belts to pantyhose—and there is a string of white gravel road which snakes down the grass and clay embankment to the store's entrance, in front of which is an island bearing two antiquated gas pumps that thud and whorl as they pull the fuel from the storage tanks beneath the earth.

Turning west down 16 and into the village of Sun puts into view the Post Office on the right, its redbrick facade faded and glare-hot in the white September sun. Just past the Post Office is the Marshal's

Office, a small square building built of faded pink cinderblocks with a cracked brown door and an old hitchingrail beneath the window where the Marshal's car is parked. Across the street from the Marshal is the City Hall with its still-hanging Confederate flag, windtorn, flapping lugubriously against its rusty and decrepit pole.

The Big Hammock Baptist Church is planted at the far western end of the village, a good mile past the last manmade structure and separated from town by the high and serried pines which stand in rows as if a cornfield. The side door of the church gives way to a narrow peagravel walkway which leads from the building and to a white and brown mobile home belonging to Pastor Varner, one of the first charismatics to enter the Southern Baptist Church as such and who came in from Mobile Alabama some twenty-five years ago to start up his church and build a congregation of Godfearing Christians. The steeple, at whose peak sits a high white steel cross which casts its shadow over Varner's trailer every afternoon, can be seen from almost any point in town, save for the places whose view is limited by pines or weedgrowth. The steeple's height is challenged only by the rise of the village's watertower which juts above the pines some hundred and seventy two feet, a large metal dome, gray-white, with the words Sun Louisiana painted across its riveted facade.

The residents of Sun live off clay and gravel roads which jut out from Highway 16 and into the woods which surround the town and separate it from Enon and Bogalusa and Mississippi. The oldtimers who sit out front of Shorty's all day, who watch the comings and goings of everyone in town and those who are just passing through, while smoking from corncob pipes, who talk about the folks who live here as if they're all related, say it's nice to be cut off like this. That they like it.

But the drought has been causing a problem. A big one. The Mayor Slocum has begun to warn the townsfolk that this thing might not end for a while yet and they might want to consider other options. But for most of the residents of Sun there are no options. There is only this place. And if it dies they must die with it.

Doyle

It's raining in New Orleans now. But not hard. The steam rises from the streets and there's a thin veil-like mist over everything, and the people walk faster, their clothes damp, hair dripping. Sweat and rain. It's quiet and the sun hangs high in the sky as if hung by strings there, beating through the few rainclouds that are moving southward now, across the Mississippi River, away from where they're needed further north, their gray-white tendrils whisping behind them like chimneysmoke as they float, drawing odd shadows over the bright brown surface of the water.

The noise from the riverfront has not ceased either—the steam organs on the riverboats, the beggars, peddlers hawking their wares, the couples in love, they're all there still. It is as if the rain does not exist for them, so they continue with their business, their rituals, as if nothing out of the ordinary is taking place.

Two couples are walking side by side. They are laughing and smoking cigarettes, a fat cloud of smoke follows them, and they, like everyone else here, seem oblivious to this rain. The two women are wearing cut-off shorts and high heels, tight scoopneck shirts, and long dirtyblonde ponytails. People stare at them as they walk by.

The men who are walking in front of these girls are talking to each other, blowing cigarette smoke into the air behind them, where the women are. They are not laughing.

One of the men says: I think it's about time we get outta here.

We been here for twelve years. Why do you wanna leave now?

I dont know, but I just got a bad feeling.

Well, what do you propose we do with them? He flicks a thumb back at the women.

I doubt they'll miss us.

Like hell they wont.

We'll take em then.

Shit, he says. Then he blows out a cloud of smoke. The women are still laughing about something.

They keep walking, the men silent now, the women laughing still. The cessation of rain has brought on the heat full force now and the men are irritated. The women dabble their faces with Kleenexes and drop the pink and brown tissues onto the steaming sidewalk.

Hey, dont drop those on mah front porch. A man is leaning over from his wheelchair and is picking up the tissues and putting them into a plastic bucket now with some loose change and wrinkled dollar bills sprinkled about the bottom.

The women stop. Giggling. Sorry, mister, one of them says.

Hey, it's okay, most people dont know this mah front porch. Just look like a sidewalk to em.

The two men in front stop and turn around. One of them says: Come on.

Wait, wait, the man in the wheelchair says, yall look like newlyweds. Am I right?

The women laugh. The men walk over to them.

I member when I was a newlywed. Got married right heah in the city. Over at Saint Augustine choich. That's mah wife over there, he says sibilantly. He points a cracked brown finger across the sidewalk to a metal parkbench where a woman sits sleeping, stooped over under a black plastic yardbag to stay dry, even though the rain has stopped, a small green purse at her thigh.

Hey baby. She doesnt look up. Hey. The man takes his cigarette and flicks it at the woman, the damp butt plucking her in the chest. She wakes, rolls her eyes around in her head, then picks up the cigarette gratefully and starts smoking it. She doesnt say anything.

Come on, one of the men says. He pulls at one of the girl's arms. They all start to walk away now.

Wait pops. I wanna play a song for yall. Just one song.

Uh-huh, one of the men says. They've seen this before.

We aint givin you no money.

It aint givin. My old man always said I gots to work for what I want, and that's what I gonna do. I wanna play you a song, and then you jist give me what you think it's woith.

No. We're in a hurry. Sorry.

You pretties look like you wanna heah a song. Come on, just one song.

One of the women says: All right. Sing us one then.

The men flick their halfsmoked cigarettes into the brown river and shove their hands into their jeanspockets. Angry now.

Then the crippled bum wheels himself closer to the two men and two women, pushing the bill of his cap up on his forehead, exposing one milky eye and another one bloodshot and jaundice-yellow. The four teeth in his mouth are chalky and orange and his hair explodes in greasy black puffs from either side of his filthy cap. He stands up on two pencil-thin legs, his kneecaps white and cracked and ashen, his shins speckled with sores and oozing pus. He is wearing khaki pants that have been cut into shorts, and his mismatched green and white socks dangle pathetically over the tops of his stretched loafers. He juts out his bony and quivering hand.

Name's Luscious.

The women look at his hand, step back.

I aint gonna bite. I aint got rabies, he says. A spray of saliva lands on one of the women's arms as he makes the difficult S sound, when his parched tongue struggles to find its place among the four jagged and sporadic teeth and the hollow caves in his rotting gums where teeth once were. The woman wipes her arm against her shirt.

But she still doesnt take his hand. The old man hobbles for a second then sits back down in his wheelchair. The chair rolls back toward the river, which is behind him, a fat string of water. Then the chair stops rolling. The women move nervously. The men just wait for this to be over. They've seen this too many times.

Okay, okay, well we dont have to shake, ladies, Luscious says now. But I still gonna keep mah promise. And I gonna do somethin that pretty much gonna amaze you. That's mah word.

The women are quiet, watching him.

One of the men lights another cigarette, waits.

Luscious says: Okay. Now I want you to look at these buckets I got heah. See em?

The women nod.

Okay, well they look like regular buckets to you, I'm sure. But I'm bout to turn them into musical instruments.

He points to the two buckets that he has now pulled in front of his wheelchair, one yellow and one blue. Another blue one which is jutted against a lamppost is the one where Luscious tossed the women's used tissues, and it is the one with the money in it.

From next to his gaunt thigh the old man pulls out two chipped drumsticks and spins them around in his hand. One falls.

It's hell gettin old, he says. Hell. Dont let it happen to you if you can void it, he says. He bends over painfully and picks up the stick.

Now, I'm gonna turn these ordinary buckets into musical instruments right before your eyes. But I'm gonna need you to help me. Which one a you wants to help me?

One of the women steps forward. Luscious hands her a drumstick. Can you keep a beat? he asks her.

Sure, she says.

What's your name? he says.

She says: it's Courtney.

Okay then Miss Courtney, I need you to tap out this beat for me. It's like this: one and two and three and four. Like that, over and over. You think you can do that?

Sure, she says. She takes the stick and taps out the beat against the bucket. One and two and three and four.

Luscious lets her tap for a couple of measures, then he begins to bang his bucket, singing When the Saints Go Marching In, himself serving both the call and the response and stumbling and stuttering over the words, but making every effort he still has left in his forsaken bones to get it right:

> We are travlin in the footsteps
> Of those who gone before
> And we'll all be reunited
> On a new and sunlit shore
> Oh when the saints go marchin in
> Oh when the saints go marchin in
> Lord how I want to be in that number
> When the saints go marchin in
> And when the sun refuse to shine
> And when the sun refuse to shine
> Lord how I want to be in that number
> When the sun refuse to shine
> And when the moon turns red with blood
> And when the moon turns red with blood
> Lord how I want to be in that number
> When the moon turns red with blood
> Oh when the trumpet sounds its call
> Oh when the trumpet sounds its call
> Lord how I want to be in that number
> When the trumpet sounds its call
> Some say this world of trouble
> Is the only one we need
> But I'm waitin for that mornin
> When the new world is revealed.

When Luscious finishes Courtney hands him back his drumstick, then both of the women stand there quietly for a minute and then they start to clap and laugh and then they reach into their tight pockets for some change to throw into Luscious's bucket. But he's not ready to let them go yet.

Hey, he says, I got a riddle for you. It's free, and you can share it with all your friends at home.

We really gotta get going, the other woman says, looking at the two men still waiting.

It'll just take a second, Luscious says, and I promise it will be woith it.

And now Courtney drops a five dollar bill into the bucket.

Let's go, one of the men says.

Wait, Courtney says, I want to hear this joke.

It aint a joke, sweetie, it's a riddle, Luscious says, standing again. Hobbling. He leans in close, his rotten breath hot and damp on her arm and neck. She steps back.

It goes like this: Two woids. Both begin with C. Both have six letters. And both woids mean exactly the same thing. Now here's the clues: the man who make it, he dont want it, the man who buy it, he dont need it, and the man who got it, he dont even know he got it. What is it?

The women look at each other. They think over the puzzle that has just been put before them by this grotesque man as if a guardian to some sacred gates leading to their eternal salvation.

Luscious sits back into his wheelchair. Proudly. He grabs his grizzled chin and smiles up at them. The chair rolls a couple of inches closer toward the river again. The women move forward with it out of instinct.

Give up? Luscious says.

I dont know it, Courtney says.

What about you? Luscious asks the other woman.

I give up, she says.

What about you fellers? he says, pointing at the two men who are still waiting impatiently for when they can all just walk away from this.

They turn away, put their backs to him, the river. They look toward the levee and the erratic skyline of the French Quarter.

Well, here it is, Luscious says. It's a coffin and a casket. See?

The women laugh.

See? The man who make it dont want it, the man who buy it dont need it and the man who got it is dead so he dont even know he got it. And both them woids begin with a C and both have six letters.

Ahh, neat, the other woman says. That's really neat.

Now you got somethin you can share with your friends. See, Luscious always keep his promise.

The other woman drops a few quarters into the blue bucket, and the men begin moving. The women follow them. And Luscious tells them thank you and to come back to see him. The organ music from the riverboat starts up fifty yards downriver, so the couples dont hear the dilapidated man's last few words. They walk over the levee and down the stairs onto South Peters Street, crossing over onto Jackson Square, then Pirates Alley, the St Louis Cathedral looming over them, a shadow as they balance over the large stones in the walkway leading to their apartment.

The regulars at a nearby cafe drinking beer from tall glasses look at them as they walk into the building.

See how they're watching us? one of the men says, the one who was talking about leaving.

So what? the other one says.

I dont like it, Travis, that's all I'm sayin.

Grow a pair, Doyle, that's all I'm sayin. We aint leavin.

They walk inside, the girls following behind them.

But tomorrow they'll be gone, all of them, heading north across Lake Pontchartrain, over whose granite-flat surface these same two men had traveled south some twelve years ago on their way in from Saint Louis.

September 3 1987

Tuck

He had hitched. Tuck was riding back home to his wife and his land and he had planned to make things right and to be good to her and not think about that whore who was still somewhere in New Orleans probably screwing somebody else by now. He didnt care. He cared about his wife now and he wanted to see her, to hold her. He was a new man.

The fellow who picked him up was driving a small truck, its bed littered with hay and empty bags of horsefeed, their pullstrings slashing at the wind like whips. The man was chainsmoking from a damp pack of Camel cigarettes and he was pitching the halfsmoked butts out of the window. He was heading east on I-10 and had picked Tuck up at the Shell station off Esplanade and had gotten onto the interstate, slamming his palm against the dash until the truck hit sixty miles per hour, the other cars streaming past him. Horns blaring.

They were on the twinspans, going over Lake Pontchartrain and toward Slidell, when the man finally started talking.

So what's on the Northshore? the man asked.

My wife, Tuck said.

The man looked at him. He blew out a spray of lungsmoke.

Can I have one of those? Tuck pointed to the pack of cigarettes on the dash. The man picked it up and aimed it at Tuck's hand. He shook out a cigarette.

Thanks, Tuck said.

The man lit Tuck's cigarette, then took one for himself and lit it off the burning cigarette he had in his hand. Tuck rolled his window down halfway.

The men rode in silence and they were driving over the lake and about to get off the bridge.

I'm not goin no futher than Slidell, you know? the man said.

Hey, I appreciate any bit you can take me. I can get another ride easy.

Then Tuck thought about his land. He tried to imagine it now. He couldnt. He looked out at the lake, the high sun to his right, throwing down a long white rectangle of light onto the flat brown water and he thought about how he met his wife, what his life had been like then and it seemed like another life altogether, the past a slow dripping of memories and separated events until some day a pool of them has formed and when you look down you see it at your feet and you have to reckon with it—you either step right over it or if it's too big you walk right through it and hope you dont drown in it. Tuck closed his eyes, remembering now:

The sun had been hanging in the sky for two hours, a gleaming plate just above the tree line so that it looked as if it were resting there, not quite ready to go all the way up yet. This is what Tuck had felt like too, so he sat down in a sticky plastic lawn chair in his yard and he pushed away the mangy lab who had been sleeping under it. The dog cowered off and slithered into the shade under Tuck's small house as Tuck opened his second beer that morning.

He was a prizefighter then. This earlymorning drinking had become a ritual for him a few years ago after he had lost a fight and woke up the next morning in a haze of pain. The beers, he found, were the only thing that helped. Tuck closed his eyes and held the bottle to his forehead, removing it only to take a sporadic swig from its cool glass rim.

The crunch of gravel in his driveway made him sit up. The dog had come out from underneath the house now and it was looking in the direction of the front yard and then a car door opened and closed and the dog ran toward it.

Tuck couldnt see from his lawn chair who it was in his drive, but he had a pretty good guess. This guess was confirmed by a man's voice: Tuck. Hey Tuck. You out here?

Tuck didnt bother to call out. His head was pounding too hard. He got up and walked around to the front yard where Graham Cooper, his manager, was standing on the crooked and rotting porch. The dog was sniffing Graham's pants.

I'm right here, Tuck said.

Graham turned and nearly fell on a loose plank. He caught himself and put a sweaty hand on the dog's head for balance. Then he said: Man, I been looking all over for you. You didnt stick around long enough after the fight last night to hear the good news. You—

Hold on a second, will you? Tuck said. Come out back with me, why dont you? You can tell me about it over a beer. You want one?

It's eight thirty in the morning for chrissake. Graham was coming down the steps now. He said: And I'd think after getting your head thumped on by Cash Jackson for forty-five minutes last night, you'd have your—

Jesus man, what did you come here for?

Tuck started walking back to his chair in the yard. Graham followed him. You remember Mr Wickers, right? he said. That promoter from Atlanta?

Yeah.

He was at your fight last night.

So? Tuck sat down, pointed to another chair for Graham to sit in.

So, Graham said, sitting now, Wickers has got this boy from Meridian—a real promising fighter, he says. He's got a lot of talent, this kid. But he needs some publicity if he's going to make Wickers any money. That's where you come in.

Uh-huh.

You see, you got a name for yourself. Folks know you. They recognize you. So if you jump in the ring with this kid—Memphis, he's called, Memphis O'Connor—and if you put on a good show and go down nice and hard, me and you stand to make a lot of money. I'm talking enough for you to retire on. For good.

Tuck was quiet. He was busy peeling the label off his bottle, letting the thin strips of paper float down to his feet like little silver-flecked feathers.

Graham looked at him.

After a few seconds, Tuck looked up. Let me just get this straight, he said. You're asking me to throw a fight just so we can help out this asshole Wickers and some punk kid who I dont even know?

It'd help us too. It's not like we're rolling around in cash.

Tuck threw back the rest of his beer. He dropped the bottle onto the ground and thought for a minute. So how much is a lot of dough exactly?

Graham looked at him. Eight. Nine maybe.

Christ. How the hell you expect me to retire on that? That's barely enough to get me through the year.

Well it's the best—hell, it's the only offer you got right now. So I suggest you take it. You can always invest the money. Live off the interest. People do it all the time.

Tuck sighed. He stood and then he rolled his head from side to side as if it were a bowling ball wedged between his shoulders. He put his fists into the small of his back and stretched. The dog was at his feet again.

All right, I'll do it, Tuck said, putting his hand on the dog's back. Just tell me when.

Graham looked at the ground.

What? Tuck said. When do I have to fight?

Well, that's the only bad part. Wickers wants you and Memphis in the ring tomorrow night. I told you he dont want to waste any time with this kid.

Christ. Tuck pushed the dog away with his boot.

Graham stood up. He said: Well I dont really see where it makes that much difference. All you got to do is dance around this kid for a few rounds, get in one or two good ones, let him get in a few, and bam, go down. Get paid. Then go home.

Is the kid gonna know the fight's fixed?

No. He'll think it's for real. So you gotta watch yourself, you know. Be careful.

Uh-huh, Tuck said.

After Graham's car had disappeared down the driveway, lurching over the holes and leaving a large red-orange dustcloud behind it, Tuck lumbered back into his house. His head felt like a balloon that someone kept blowing air into and that at any second would burst.

He walked into the kitchen and stood in front of the refrigerator and pressed his forehead against the cool door. Then he opened it and grabbed another beer.

Then Tuck walked to his bedroom running his hand along the wainscoting that lined the walls. The little cracks between each plank felt rough, uneven, like they could cut his hand if he wasnt careful. Tuck moved his hands in front of his face and looked at them.

The room was dark, but he could see that his knuckles were still badly swollen from last night. His fingers seemed to be twisted up and going in different directions. They had been broken so many times. He wondered how they'd feel for the fight. It didnt matter. He could go down quick, get this business over with. Tuck took a pull from the brown bottle. Swallowed.

He stood there in his bedroom. He turned on the light and then he sat on the bed and grabbed his keys from the nightstand. Last night's purse of three hundred and seventy-five dollars was rolled compactly up into the empty light socket of his bedside lamp. Tuck removed the lampshade with his left hand and with his right, reached into the bulbless socket and grabbed the roll of twenties, tens, and ones. Then he stuffed it down his boot and left the room, flicking off the light on his way out.

The cab of his truck smelled like sweat and motor oil. Old hay. He had a horse in the yard which he fed by filling up the bed of his truck with the hay and letting the animal eat from it whenever it pleased. A makeshift trough. When Tuck used the truck, he would always pull out fast so that any remaining hay would fall into a pile in the yard. It didnt matter. The truck still always had that smell to it.

Tuck rolled down the window. He jolted the truck forward to shake out the hay and as he was easing onto the driveway, the dog ran toward the truck and stood below the driver's side window. It looked up at Tuck. Tuck looked at the dog.

Come on girl. Jump in. Tuck pointed a thumb to the rusty bed, still covered with a dull yellow blanket of hay. The dog went behind the old

Chevy and leaped onto the open tailgate, fanning her hind legs until she was up and peering over the side of the truck, her tongue falling from her mouth, panting.

He lumbered the old truck down the drive and onto Highway 16 and then turned onto Highway 21 and drove northeast toward Mississippi. Tuck stopped in Bogalusa for gas, then got back on 21 and crossed into Mississippi, slowing down just outside of Poplarville. Then he had to stop again. A girl was in the road. She was walking south along the centerline with two brownpaper grocery bags in her hands. She looked like an apparition. Tuck pulled the truck onto the shoulder and got out.

Mam? He couldnt see her face, but she was slugging along as if her shoes were weighted down with stones. Can I give you a hand with them groceries?

The girl stopped and turned. She looked up at Tuck. Her face was young and smooth and almost perfectly round. Her long brown hair hung in wisps over her eyes, some loose strands brushing at her small nose like soft tendrils. She placed the bags she was holding down onto the hot cracked pavement and raised her fingers to her face, brushing away the hair from her eyes and tucking it under the dark blue baseball cap she was wearing.

These aint groceries, she finally said. They're all my belongings.

She couldnt have been more than twenty-three or four, but walking like that, she had looked so old. Worn out.

Well, Tuck said, if you dont mind me askin, why are you walkin in the middle of the highway like this? You tryin to get run over?

Sorry, the girl said, picking up her bags and walking toward Tuck now. She placed the bags at his feet and removed her cap, revealing more of her young and beautiful face. She smiled and stuck out her hand. I'm Magdalene Bell, she said.

I'm Tuck. Pleased to meet you. He took her hand into his.

What happened? the girl said, feeling Tuck's swollen fingers. You been in a accident?

No, he said, I'm a fighter. A professional fighter. A boxer.

The girl considered this, then let go of Tuck's hand. Who's your dog? she said, looking to the back of the truck. Tuck was still thinking about his hands. It took him a minute to change track. His brain felt as swollen and beat up as his knuckles.

Um. Oh, her. Yeah, she's just a stray came to the house one day. All I done was feed her once, she aint left since. The dog was halfway out the truck now, licking and sniffing the girl's face.

Say, where were you headed, anyway? Tuck said. Walkin in the highway like that by yourself?

Well, I'm going somewhere. Not quite sure exactly yet. You think maybe you could give me a lift?

You dont even know me, Tuck said. How do you know I'm not a murderer or a ex-convict?

Oh, I can just tell. It's in your eyes. She put her hat back on. I can tell a lot from someone's eyes, she said.

She went back to her bags. She picked them up and walked around the front of the truck to the passenger side.

Tuck told the dog to sit down, then climbed into the cab. He reached over and unlocked the passenger door. The girl climbed in, placed her bags on the floorboard.

Tuck started the engine. So where is it that you're going? he said.

The girl took off her hat again, let her hair fall beyond her shoulders. She rolled down the window. Wherever you can take me's fine. I just need to get far away from here.

Well, I'm headed to Meridian, but it looks like you was goin in the opposite direction. I dont know if I'll be of much help.

No, anywhere is fine so long as it aint here.

Tuck put the truck into gear and it lurched forward.

After they had been driving for a while, Tuck asked the girl why she had been walking in the road like that.

She said: Well, my daddy died last week. I aint got no one else here.

Oh, I'm sorry, Tuck said.

It's okay. He used to hit on me anyway, do all kinds of other stuff too. When he died, I aint had no reason to stay. Cept the house he left behind. But I sold that. To his brother. My Uncle Ray John. He gave me cash for it.

Hm, Tuck said. I hope you aint carrying that with you. Or if you are, it's in a safe place.

It is, she said.

Then they were silent. Tuck fooled with the radio.

As the old Chevy passed through Poplarville heading north toward Meridian, Tuck rolled his window up so he could light a cigarette. He offered one to the girl, but she told him no. Tuck put the pack on the seat in the space between them. The girl looked down at it. Then she looked back up and out of the windshield at the buildings slipping past on both sides of them. A hardware. A postoffice. A secondhand store.

This is it right here, the girl said and she stuck her finger out the window and pointed at a bulky, gray-brick structure on their right. This is where I want to get off.

Tuck looked at her and then he pulled the truck into one of the empty spaces in front of the building. I thought this is where you was comin from in the first place. Dont you wanna go further away?

Well, I got somethin I got to take care of here. Somethin I forgot earlier. I'll be okay.

Tuck looked at her eyes. Pitiful. Then Magdalene Bell leaned over and kissed him on the cheek.

Thanks, she said.

She smiled and touched Tuck's hand. I appreciate your help, she said. You're welcome.

The girl patted his arm and grabbed her bags and hopped from the Chevy's oily-smelling cab and Tuck watched her as she waved to the dog in the back and walked into the building. Then Tuck pulled onto the road. Heading north again toward Meridian.

All right, here we are, the man driving the truck was saying. Slidell.

Tuck opened his eyes and looked out the window. He looked at the man. The man was smiling at him.

Thanks, Tuck said. I really do appreciate this.

The driver had stopped the truck now in front of a gas station. Aint a big deal, he was saying. Happy I could help. And I'm sure that wife a yours'll appreciate it too. This aint a time when a body wants to be alone. Specially a woman. Times like these is when a woman wants her man around.

Thanks, Tuck said for the second time.

December 21 1987

Vermena

What we had all heard about Miss Tucker was that she aint had no family of her own cept for some mean daddy who used to hit her all the time and then dropped dead all of a sudden. She was a few years youngern Tuck. And she just come down here from Poplarville with him one day. Tuck had told some folks that he met her up there while he was still fightin and fell in love with her and decided to bring her back here to Sun to live.

To tell the truth none of us was that shocked by it neither. Tuck was like that, you understand, always doin things spur of the moment. So we just accepted her into the town and treated her with respect like we would anyone else.

And none of us was surprised neither when Tuck took off to New Orleans with that little tramp he met at The Horse a few years later. We felt sorry for Miss Tucker, but we didnt know what to do for her. She had a little bit a money from Tuck, plus she had the house and the land which Tuck had done paid off after that last fight a his some years ago. So really there wasnt nothin we coulda done for her, except maybe just lend a ear to her if she wanted somebody to talk to about it. But she never did.

She just come into town every now and then for things and still smiled and said hi just the same as before, as if nothin at all had ever happened. So we smiled back and said hi back and prayed for that poor little girl every time we thought about her or every time her name came up in conversation. Then that drought came and then Joe Wallace showed up in town lookin for work and everything just went to hell.

We all figured the two a them was out there in them woods and in that house shackin up, but what could we do or say about it? Look what Tuck done did to her. It wouldnt a been right for us to go judgin on her, even though Pastor Varner, he be preachin about sin and hellfire ever Sunday and tellin us it was our Christian duty to expel them very things from our town, and that it was the existence of them very things that was why God was holdin back the rain from us for so long. That God wasnt about to replenish a piece of His earth that was so mired in sin and lies, that He might as well just let it die, boot us from it like He done Adam and Eve from the Great Garden when they done sinned.

But we still didnt know what to do about it at first. Like I been sayin all along, we had us some bigger fishes to fry up with the drought goin on than to sit and worry about that. But then some folks, they started talkin. Started thinkin that maybe Varner was right. Started speculatin that maybe we was the cause of this drought, that God would put some rain on us if we'd just see our ways for what they was and go break up this business we suspected was goin on over at the Tucker place.

So one night after Bible study and after Pastor Varner brought some demons from a coupla folks by layin his hand on they forehead and speakin in tongues until they went all limp and then started flappin around on the ground like electric wires done come off they pole, a coupla us got together and talked about goin out to the place and havin us a talk with Miss Tucker and Joe Wallace.

Yes we was gonna exercise some demons of our own. And we was damn sure gonna get some rain on this place come hell or high water as the sayin goes. We just had to show God that we was worthy to receive His gifts. By lookin Satan straight in the eye and stompin him down from whence he came with the divine power of the Good Word.

September 3 1987

Jebediah

I walked into this river to be saved when I was twelve years old. The water was ambercolored and cool on my legs and chest. I was going to be baptized in the name of Jesus Christ the Lord. But this is what happened instead:

Pastor Varner had just come to Sun from Alabama to start up his church here and he was only twenty three and he had some people there from the church already waiting on the riverbank. They were wearing dark suits and dark glasses. One of them had a white towel to dry me off when I came out of the water. Reborn. The pine trees towered overhead and cast long shadows across the white sand, pure and cool beneath our feet. My mother was there, but no one else from my family. She blotted her cheeks with a handkerchief. She was crying.

But I was ready. I had been called.

I rolled up my pantslegs to my knees. My calves and my feet were turning almost purple since the blood wasnt going to them now. My cinched pantscuffs were cutting off the circulation. Pastor Varner held me by the forearm and led me into the river, two other men from the congregation following us, Brother Gaylon and Brother Bill. The cold water encapsulated first our legs and then our thighs as we walked in. A branch floated past us and down the long string of water heading south, a black fissure in the smooth brown line of water.

Come on son, Pastor Varner was saying. Let go of yourself and come to the Lord.

We kept walking out until the water was up to our stomachs then just under our chests. Pastor Varner's dark suit turned darker where it was wet and the white shirt he had on was tan where the silt from the river stuck to it. My shirt too felt tighter and I could see my flesh through it the more wet it became. The flesh on my arms prickled at the cold.

We stopped just in the middle of the river, the sun coming through the trees now like slats of light on the purling water, looking like prisonbars around me and Pastor Varner and Brothers Gaylon and Bill. In his right hand Pastor Varner held his blackleather Bible and a white handkerchief up and above the water and he held my arm still with his left hand. His grip had gotten tighter as the current pulled at our bodies from underneath. Brother Gaylon and Brother Bill stood on either side of us.

The crowd on the riverbank waited silently and watched us standing in the river as Pastor Varner read and read, furiously turning the pages as he went and finally saying: Repent, and be baptized in the name of Jesus Christ for the remission of sins, and ye shall receive the gift of the Holy Ghost.

He placed his hand on my forehead and gently tilted my head up so that I could see the trees pointing up toward the sky and Brother Gaylon and Brother Bill took hold of my shoulders and I started to take in a breath so I could hold it as I went under and just as I did I felt their hands push me down into the water and I felt the rush of it cold in my mouth and throat and lungs closing up around the swirl like two fists now and my legs and arms flailing and them letting me up just as fast but my lungs already filled with water and me coughing now as I came up trying to breathe.

Sparks of light bounced across my eyes as I tried to stand up but couldnt seem to get my footing in the soft riverbottom and Brother Gaylon wiping my face with a towel now. And then darkness. A swallowing black.

And that's all I remember. Except for when I was unconscious and in that darkness like a deep sleep I saw Jesus and he wouldnt look at me, wouldnt save me. I felt my body reaching out to him but then he was gone and it was just the dark again. I had not been saved.

When I came to I was lying in the sand and everyone was standing over me looking down and I saw my mother and Pastor Varner was still praying over me that my sins be washed away and then I turned my head to the side and expelled the rest of the water that was in my body.

That was in 1964. It would be another nineteen years before Jesus would come to me and I would be saved for good.

Magdalene

And now Magdalene is thinking and she is saying this to Joe Wallace too:

When I first met Tuck was right after Daddy died. I just sold the house to my uncle and I was leaving Poplarville for good. Or thought I was. I didnt have a car. Daddy's truck was all but dead too so I just gave it to Uncle Ray John with the house. Included it in the selling price. He said he'd fix the thing up for me, that it wouldnt take much work, but I told him he could just keep it. I didnt want nothing to do with anything of Daddy's now, but I didnt tell that to Uncle Ray John. I guess he just thought I was being nice.

The things I owned fit perfectly in two brownpaper grocery bags and that's all I had with me when I headed out the house and down the road away from town. I was heading south toward Louisiana, no place in particular in mind, just moving, walking, trying to get far from where me and Daddy lived. I had been walking for a couple of hours when this truck, heading north, came toward me. It pulled over a little bit onto the shoulder and then a man got out and told me his name was Tuck Tucker and that he was a boxer and then he asked me if I needed a ride, that he could bring me into town even though that wasnt the way I was headed.

He seemed nice enough so I took him up on his offer, told him he had kind eyes, the kind one could trust. So we got into his truck and headed north. We had a nice enough conversation and something about it got me to thinking about the money I had on me. The money from Daddy's house. I asked Tuck to drop me off in town in front of the bank and he did and that's where I put all that money. It's still there too. I never told Tuck about it, so he never had the chance to spend it on his drinking. A couple of times now since this drought started up, I thought about driving up there to take it out, but figured it's best where it is. Collecting interest. Staying safe.

I've seen two of our animals die since the drought started— Tuck's dog that he left when he took off a few months ago and now that horse, which I cant even bury properly. And I cant feel right about asking you to take care of it. You've done so much for me already. But I dont plan on letting us die, so if it comes down to it, we'll just have to drive up to Poplarville ourselves to get that money. Make a life someplace else. I dont feel beholden to this place at all really.

So anyway Tuck came back after his fight he had in some barn in Meridian that night and found me in town at a little diner, sat down with me, him all bruised up and sweaty, and we just started talking. He said he lost his fight on purpose that night: for the money, and that he was retired from fighting now. We talked about where he was from in Louisiana and he told me Sun and that he wanted to take this retirement money he just got from losin his fight and start up a little farm there. Make an honest living. Maybe even start a family too.

Next thing I know I'm here in Sun living with this man I hardly know but making a good go of it. I really liked him then. We got married at the Justice of the Peace, a couple of the oldtimers from out front of Shorty's coming in to serve as witnesses, and for a while, things were okay. Tuck bought that tractor over there that you've been usin and a Bushhog, cleared some land, and we started making plans. But it wasnt long before he started staying out nights, then disappeared altogether, leaving me to tend to this land and with this drought and the folks in town who seem to have nothing better to think about than what I am doing and who I am doing it with. I guess you could say I'm worn out.

Tuck

The next car to stop and pick up Tuck was coming down Old Spanish Trail and was heading toward I-10 and pulled over to the side of the road when its driver saw Tuck walking there with his thumb out.

Where you headed? the driver said.

Round Bogalusa.

I can take you as far as Covington. Get in.

Tuck looked at the car. There were no doors. Two yellow ropes hung in loose curves from one end of each doorframe to the other, forming a sort of web at the openings.

Just lift em up and crawl in, the driver said.

Tuck separated the ropes, threw in his duffel, and climbed into the car as if he were climbing into a boxing ring again. He looked at the driver. Then he put out his hand.

I'm Tuck.

Puckett. Pleased to meet you. The man shook Tuck's hand and looked at him. Tuck could see from where he was now sitting in the low passenger seat of the rusty Camaro that the right half of this man's face was sagging as if there were no bone beneath it. As if the right side of his jaw had been removed completely.

The left side of the man's mouth stretched up into a grin. He stubbed out his cigarette against the cracked and sweating dash, threw it out of the doorhole, and put the car into gear, merging onto I-10 at sixty five.

When the driver hit ninety, he reclined his seat a bit, then yelled over the wind that was rushing into the car: So I'm goin to see my kids. Havent seen em in nine years. My ex-wife's been tryin to keep em from me, but she caint hide em forever.

Tuck didnt say anything. He could hardly hear the man over the windrush.

Then the man said: So what's in Bogalusa? You live out thataway?

No actually it's Sun where I live. I'm goin home to my wife. Tuck was yelling too now.

The man nodded at this, then gripped the steering wheel hard as he rounded the on-ramp to get on I-12 and screeched the car around the curve at seventy. Tuck was holding onto the sideropes that were barely keeping him from falling out of the car as they made the curve and went up the ramp. He closed his eyes. The driver was yelling at his car now, pounding the dash.

Come on Bubba. He was yelling out of one side of his halfjaw like some deranged comicbook villain. If Tuck had been a man of God, he'd have prayed then.

Then the car was on I-12 heading west and Puckett brought the Camaro back up to ninety. He weaved in and out of traffic, honking and cursing and spitting at everyone in his path. Tuck just closed his eyes.

Joe

This guy in prison told me a story once about how he used to hump his bed when he was a kid. He knew it was sick but now that he was in prison he took to doing it again. Said he just cut a hole right in the mattress. With a piece of metal he broke off one of the shower stalls. Just cut the fabric and dug out the material. Right plumb in the middle so he could get to it.

At night he'd work his hand in the hole and bend the wire mesh that was inside the mattress back and forth until the pieces broke off. Then he threw em away piece by piece.

Once he had the hole all cleaned out he took a fistful of Vaseline and coated the hole up with it thick like candlewax. He said the first night was like losin his virginity all over again. Said it made his legs go numb. It got to where we could all hear him at night goin to town on that mattress. Just doing it all night long it seemed. Kept all of us who lived in the barracks awake half the night. Some of the guys that slept right next to him got fed up with the noise after about a week and one of them put some Borax from out the laundry in that damned hole. Just sprinkled it onto the Vaseline so he wouldnt see it. Well come night when he got himself into that hole and started going to town on it, it wasnt long before he jumped up hollering and screaming and holding on to himself, running to the end of the barracks and almost plumb into the wall.

The next morning the guards found him killed. Somebody had stabbed him. Had that piece of metal from the shower stall that he used to cut his mattress with stuck right through his neck.

No one ever did find that mattress either. I guess somebody liked it better than their own and traded up before the guards came in the next morning to collect the dead man's things. To return it all to his family, if he even had one, or if they would even want to claim his things in the first place. I never found out.

Jebediah

Because Jebediah Willie had long ago sensed the end, it made little sense for him to wait for it to take him, to waste away waiting for it to come. But for his awareness he was grateful. Yet he saw no need to warn anyone else, felt blessed in fact that only he had seen the signs of the end, recognized them for what they were. For they were not easy to discern. Signs. Indicators of the second coming. None of this came easy he knew.

And this recent drought only confirmed his suspicions. So he had set up a little encampment along the Bogue Chitto River under the Highway 21 bridge and had planned to ride out the storm of all storms until Jesus Christ Himself lifted his soul into the sky and carried him toward His infinite bounty.

And this is where he is now and has been for several months. Waiting. Fishing in the shallow and receding waters of the now-evaporating Bogue Chitto River, the skein of smoke from the small campfire in front of his tent a spire now whispering under the trusses of the bridge and curling and eddying there, swirling around the gritty concrete stanchions, then settling into a thin

107

flat haze before finding its way up beyond that and over the steel siderails of the bridge so that the drivers of the cars passing overhead think that maybe their engines are overheating so they pull over at Shorty's when they get to the other side to check under their hoods, find nothing wrong, and so continue on to Bogalusa or Poplarville since no one ever stops in Sun unless summoned there from whatever place they had long ago run away to.

Jebediah walks along the banks, the white sand under his bare feet, and he looks into the brown string of water, sees his reflection, a gaunt but well-toned and darkly tanned frame, his skin now the color of oxblood leather. He is shirtless, a pair of khaki shorts barely hanging on to his protruding hipbones, from which two thin dark legs emerge, then grow into feet which seem to stab at the sand with each disdainful step he takes along the shoals, looking for fish to catch.

This is the same river in which he had been baptized some twenty-three years ago when he was only twelve years old and had almost drowned when Pastor Varner sunk his head under just as he was taking in a breath.

Jebediah holds his pole over his shoulder and looks for some glimmer in the water, some sign that he will eat soon. But sees none. Signs are never easy. You always have to be looking for them.

When he gets beyond the shadow of the bridge, the sunlight bounces off of the surface of the river in a white triangle and he stops and looks at it, catches a glint in the water, readies his pole, then realizes that this spark is a reflection from above and not his. He looks across the river toward the other bank and sees a figure staring back at him. The figure is holding something in its hands out toward Jebediah, pointing it toward him, but Jebediah cannot make it out.

Howdy, a voice calls from the other side.

And Jebediah, who hasnt spoken to nor seen anyone in months save for Pastor Varner who comes out to check on him once in a while, stabs his pole into the sand, raises his hand to his forehead to block out the sun's white glare, squints his eyes, looks at the figure on the other side and says hi back. And it is then that he sees the gray flint-colored pistolbarrel jutting out from the figure's right hand, pointed at him, fracturing the triangle of white light over the water like a nail being hammered through someone's foot or wrist.

I'm Travis, the figure says, walking into the river toward Jebediah now as if he were himself being baptized, the water wrapping itself in tiny waves around his blue boots as he walks toward this man who is waiting confusedly on the other side as if for a better more readable sign to appear.

Pastor Varner

The folks from Big Hammock are following Pastor Varner now down past Snake Jenkins Road and toward the cratered gravel drive that leads to Magdalene Tucker's house. The road is dried and cracked under their feet and they walk over the cracks carefully so their shoes wont go in. The powder that hovers around their ankles and feet is orange and the cloud seems to follow them as they make their way down the road. It looks like a dust storm.

Pastor Varner holds a beaten and blackleather Bible and a white handkerchief in his right hand and he holds it above his head as if exhorting the sky or the lank pines on either side of him with its word and his own personal paean while the ruck behind him follows in mute prayer and with arms and hands hanging like limp and dangling fish.

Tuck

I sure do appreciate the ride. Tuck climbs awkwardly out of the car and looks at the clear sky now. It sure is hot, he says.

Tell me about it, Puckett says, the limp and jawless side of his face flapping like a piece of damp leather, his words nearly aphonic and slurred and dying midbreath.

Thanks again, Tuck says.

Anytime.

Puckett revs the 383 Stroker under his rusty hoodpiece until the car itself shakes with the horsepower. He throws the lever to the brake, lets out the clutch, and disappears into a cloud of black smoke that stinks of burning rubber and hot tar. Tuck puts his hand over his mouth and turns toward the shoulder and starts walking, the gravel crunching under his boots as he rounds the curve of Highway 21 toward Waldheim. With his duffel draped over his shoulder, his thumb out, he kicks the rocks ahead of him with his boots, pointing them toward home now.

Magdalene

She is telling this to Joe now and still thinking too: I was at home when Daddy died. They called me from the landfill where he worked and told me he dropped dead, just stopped breathing. They told me the ambulance had already come and picked him up and brought him to the hospital. They said I needed to go over there and make arrangements, get his things. I hung up the phone. I sat at the kitchen table and tried to force the tears, but they wouldnt come. I thought if I cried, I'd feel better.

But I couldnt cry.

Instead I went into his room and took the filthy sheets from his bed and brought them outside. I stuffed them in the garbage can and then I grabbed some newspaper and lit it with a match. When it was burning good, I dropped it into the can with the sheets and stood in front of the midden and watched the black smoke come out and into the sky. It burned my eyes and the tears finally came. It was the best I could muster.

I had to walk to the hospital. It wasnt far, about twenty five minutes from the house. I remember thinking that he wasnt really going to be dead when I got there. That he was going to be waiting for me in a room and he was going to pull me in and pull me under the sheets with him and that he would try to get on top of me.

I almost turned around twice. But I finally got to the hospital and the nurse at the desk told me where he was when I gave her his name. She didnt say that he was dead and I almost asked her if he was or not, but figured I best go and see for myself.

I walked down the halls and finally got to the room. There was a curtain over the opening instead of a door and just as I was about to pull it back to go in, someone from inside the room pulled at it too and came out the opening, almost running into me. It was a doctor.

Miss Bell, he said.

Yes?

I just want you to know that we did everything we could in order to revive your father. But you must understand that by that point there was really not much that could be done to save him.

I nodded, although I didnt understand what he was telling me.

If you need anything, Miss Bell, please let me know. You can buzz the nurse from the room and she'll get me.

Thank you, I said.

The doctor patted me on the shoulder with his soft hand and slid out of my way. The curtain had fallen back into its place, so I pulled it open again and stepped into the room. The room was empty save for a table, a chair, and the bed where my daddy's body lay. He was on top of the sheets and he was wearing his workpants but no shirt. His skin was purple and splotchy looking and in only a few places was it its normal color—a dark tan. His hair was messy and looked much grayer than it normally did. Both of his eyes werent quite shut all the way and his mouth was open a little bit too. I walked over to him.

Daddy? I said to him.

He didnt move. He looked to be sleeping, save for his chest's not rising or falling.

Daddy, what happened to you?

He was still.

I put my hand on his chest. It felt cold and hardened. I stepped back from him. I moved to the only chair in the room and sat down.

There was a phone book on the table next to the bed. I opened it, thumbed through some of the pages, but there was no one to call.

I sat there for a while, checking his eyes or to see if his chest moved just to make sure that he wasnt really alive and was about to jump on me with all of his weight like he used to do. His body never flinched. After a half hour or so a woman came into the room and looked at me, then looked at Daddy.

She said hi to me, then put a wooden clipboard on Daddy's chest and started looking in Daddy's mouth with a little penlight. She took a pencil from her ear and wrote some things on a form on the clipboard, then stepped back. She looked at the tattoos on Daddy's chest and sucked her tongue and shook her head. Then she looked at me again and stepped out of the room.

Then another doctor came into the room and he asked me if I had any plans for the burial. He told me that I had to call someone because the room could not be tied up all night. He said he didnt mean to sound rude. He pointed to the phone book on the table and told me to take my time.

I called the first funeral home I came across and the man on the other end talked so low I couldnt hardly hear him. He said he would send someone over shortly. I sat in the chair and stared at Daddy until the curtain was pulled open again and a tall man walked into the room. He didnt look at Daddy. He looked at me and he had his hands folded and at his waist. He introduced himself in a low voice like the man on the phone had used, and he offered his condolences and told me that he was here to remove the body.

I nodded.

Then he asked me if I needed a few more minutes, that he'd be right outside, and then he pulled the curtain back and walked out. I went over to Daddy and pushed his hair back with my hand so it wouldnt look so messy and then I walked out of the room without looking back. I didnt say anything.

The tall man from the funeral home was standing in the hallway, his hands still folded, and he approached me with that slow and quiet way of his. He handed me his card and asked me to call him the next day so that we could make arrangements.

Yes sir.

Thank you mam, he said. Have a good night.

When I got home, I took everything else from the house that belonged to Daddy. Everything this time. I put it all in the front yard into a pile. I lit some more newspapers and waited until the flames got big in my hand and then I shoved the papers into the spaces between all of Daddy's things: clothes, guns, magazines, fishing tackle, milk crates full of tools, pictures of him and Mama before I was born, and I even put my own bedsheets in there too since he had desecrated those also. The fire was taller than me and some of the neighbors stood in their doorways to see what was going on.

I watched the fire until dawn when it finally died out and the smoke was thick and black and burned my throat and there was nothing left but a pile of ash and soot and Daddy's workboots and the plastic and metal things that just wouldnt take to burning. The guns too were in there still. I grabbed a stick to scrape the boots and the guns and the other things out of the burnpile and as I stood over it now pulling out his blackened and ruined things the smoke crawled into my eyes and I cried a real good cry finally. And that was it. The last of the crying I done over him.

Daddy

She would always be sayin: Daddy, Daddy, why do you do that to me?

When I'm just tryin to keep sane in this world. Get what little pleasure a man can. God begot me a daughter and I aimed I should do what I wanted with her. What with my wife gone and no other outlet for a man. She was mine. And I aint harmed her. Just taught her only what's natural to folk. The way of things. She should've been grateful.

I worked all day to keep her fed and dressed. Put her in school. Most times it'd keep me up to fourteen hours a day. Just to make ends meet. Shovelin and pushin dirt from one end of the earth to the other. Miserable work. Wouldnt wish it on the devil hisself. Feel like he wished it on me though. To this day I cant figure what I done to him to give me such a awful lot. But that's the way of things I suppose.

I'd come home covered in black dirt, lookin like some damned nigger. All you could see was my teeth and the whites around my eyes. Smelled like death had done got a grip on me. And there she'd be. Poor thing, had dinner ready, doin her homework at the table, waitin for me.

Hey Daddy, she'd say.

Hey baby.

I cooked dinner for us.

I see that.

Just like Mama.

Yep, just like your mama.

I'd be so damned hungry, I wouldnt even clean myself up. I'd just sit down and start to eatin, smellin like death and covered in filth. Shoveling the food in my mouth like the dirt in that God-forsaken landfill where I spent all day toiling in other people's waste. Damn Adam and God above for their curse. And damn Eve too for trickin him up. He should've known not to trust no woman. Always getting a man into trouble.

Just like this girl's mama: gets pregnant, has the damn thing, then takes off. Leaves me with the burden of workin and raisin a child. And I done the best I could. The best I could. That girl never went without. I went without but she never did. And that's how things was.

I'd come home, eat dinner, sit on the sofa with a beer and pass out until it was time to repeat the thing all over again the next day. But Magdalene, she started getting older.

And I kept lookin at her, God, I couldnt help it. A man's got his needs. And they gotta get met somehow. And I kept lookin and lookin, swearin that nothin would happen. But then one day it did.

She had dinner ready as usual. Sittin at the table doin her schoolwork.

Hey Daddy.

Hey baby.

We ate. And I went to the sofa stinking and black and I turned on the TV and opened a beer and drank it in one swallow and called for Magdalene to bring me another one. She did. I drank it in two swallows and called for one more. When she handed it to me, her finger touched mine just a little bit, but it was just enough to put the hairs on the back of my neck up. I pulled her to me.

Tell Daddy a story, I said.

Her eyes got a little wide, but she smiled and pulled away.

I got homework Daddy. She smiled and went back into the kitchen. Her legs were smooth and hard. I watched her walk away. I drank the beer she brought me in three quick gulps and closed my eyes.

I waited five minutes. Baby can you bring me another one?

Just a second Daddy.

She was flirting. I knew it. Just like Eve. She knew what she was doing. Eve wanted out of that Garden so damned bad and she wanted to bring Adam with her. Just couldnt do it alone. And here I was suffering the same plight as the first son of God. In my own den. I wasnt gonna have it. She brought me the beer.

Come here, I told her.

Daddy, I told you I got homework.

I didnt wait for her to turn around this time. I grabbed her soft white wrist, my black hand like some damned nigger and not me got holt of her. And I pulled her to me. She fell across my lap.

Daddy, she yelled. But not really yelled. Just kind of loud like she was callin out to me from a separate room.

I moved my hands up her shirt. She was still pulling away from me. Stop it, she was sayin. Over and over. She was breathing real heavy and sounded like she was starting to cry some so I let her go and she jumped up from my legs and ran off into the kitchen and shut off the light in there and then she ran off into her room and slammed the door behind her but I could still hear her weeping even from all the way down the hall in her room behind the closed door.

I cursed the both of us and then fell asleep.

She stayed away from me for the most part after that. But after a month or two things started getting back to normal and I knew she was just playin games with me so I decided to put an end to it right then and there.

I had a few beers in me. No food to speak of. Just beer. Magdalene had stopped makin dinner for me. I was covered in dirt and filth and stinking. I walked into her room.

She looked up from her homework. She was laying on her

stomach on her bed in her underwear. She didnt say anything. Just looked at me with those round eyes of hers.

I moved toward the bed. What are you workin on?

She didnt answer.

Schoolwork?

No answer. Just that look. She was still upset with me.

And just like that I fell onto her like a sack of horsefeed and next thing I know I was walkin out her room and closing the door behind me with her sobbin and sayin Why why why over and over, but I didnt know if she was talkin to me or to God or to herself so I pulled the door to and cursed the lot of us and our miserable and forsaken lives for good.

Doyle

This guy aint got shit worth takin, Travis says, nudging angrily at the body of Jebediah Willie with the steel tip of his turquoise boot.

Doyle is looking down at the man Travis has just shot, the blood from the man's head now turning black in the sand. Doyle looks up.

Cept for that damned truck over there, Travis is saying, pointing toward the foot of the embankment leading up to the bridge, on which an old pickup truck sits listlessly.

A total waste of bullet if you ask me, he says, spitting into the shallow amber water and stepping back into it as if putting out a fire. Let's go. The girls are still waitin up there on the bridge. Drive this here truck up there if you can start her, and I'll ditch our car in them woods. We'll see how far this thing gets us.

Then Travis walks up the marled embankment, slipping twice, but getting to the summit nonetheless and he disappears over the cement guardrail. Doyle is still standing next to the body and he puts a towel that Travis had pitched from the tent over the bleeding and mutilated head and he stands up and says he is sorry to no one, to the air, to the river half gone with drought, to God, the bridge overhead, the body that lay bleeding and desecrated by his friend's hand in a swath of dry caliche-like sand that is now going black with blood. This man's end has come, and Doyle knows that his has come now as well. He stands there silently.

Then he walks over to the dead man's truck and tries the ignition. It starts on the third turn. A puff of black smoke sprays from the tailpipe. Doyle lets the truck idle until all of the exhaust finds its way out of the engine and then he drives it toward the embankment, struggling it up to the bridge where Travis and the girls are standing carless now like three hitchhikers waiting for someone to stop and give them a ride, which he does.

Tuck

When Tuck got out of the car that had picked him up last and walked into the gravel lot in front of Shorty's, the oldtimers stared at him with a vague interest. One of them spat.

Howdy Tuck.

Howdy yourself.

It's been a while.

Yep.

Where you been? one of them said.

Another said: Earl, you know damn well he been in New Orleans. What the hell you askin him that for?

I was just tryin to make small talk, Earl said.

Hm, the other one said.

Any of you gentlemen seen my wife of late? Tuck asked.

Nossir, they mumbled. Aint seen her in a right smart long time, it seems.

How yall makin out in this drought? Tuck said.

Barely, Earl said. If it dont rain soon, I reckon we all gonna turn to dust.

That'd be the day, another one said.

Dust, Earl said, then spat.

Well I think I'm gonna head down there. See my wife. You gentlemen take care now.

Hm, Earl said.

December 21 1987

Vermena

That day we done all got together at Big Hammock and met up with Pastor Varner and walked down Highway 16 until we got to the little gravel road that led to Miss Tucker's place where she was shackin up with that Wallace boy was one I'll never forget. Like I said earlier we had done got all filled up with the Spirit the night before during meetin, folks speakin in tongues and fallin on the ground, Pastor Varner slappin they foreheads and they go to floppin on the ground like electricity was goin all through them, so we was still all full of God's fire when we started marchin our group over there the next afternoon to rid our town of Joe Wallace's and Miss Tucker's sins so that God would give us some rain.

Pastor Varner had called us sinners too for not ridding our town of this sooner, said we was just as guilty in God's eyes, that's why we was all sufferin. This was a test, he said. He said this Joe Wallace was not back here by accident, that God sent him to test us, test our moral fortitude, see if we could recognize true sin for what it was and then take the steps to rid ourselves of it. God was always testin us, he said. And true Christian folks saw these tests for what they was and made the right decision every time. Were we true Christians, he asked us. Yes, we all yelled. He asked us again. We all yelled yes again and the whole congregation broke out into furious song and speakin in tongues until not a single one of us was sittin still or had dry eyes. God had filled all of us with His Holy Spirit that night and it was still inside us as we marched on over to Miss Tucker's place come the next day.

I was carryin my Bible and so was my husband and most of the rest of them. We was prayin silently as we walked and Pastor Varner stayed in front of us and led the way.

He was readin from his Bible, holdin it up to the sky every now and again when he was recitin from memory, sayin things like: If a man be found lyin with a woman married to an husband, then they shall both of them die, both the man that lay with the woman, and the woman: so shalt thou put away evil from the land.

Amen, someone in the group shouted.

Pastor Varner kept readin and recitin, wavin his white handkerchief and sayin: If a damsel that is a virgin be betrothed unto a husband, and a man find her in the city, and lie with her, then ye shall bring them both out unto the gate of that city, and ye shall stone them with stones until they die.

Amen, we all yelled.

The damsel, because she cried not (Pastor Varner was still readin now), bein in the city, and the man, because he hath humbled his neighbor's wife: so thou shalt put away evil from among you.

Amen, we yelled.

Put away the evil among us, he yelled.

Put it away, we yelled again.

Rid ourselves of it for good.

For good, we said: and we kept marching, jubilant now.

And damned if just before we got to Miss Tucker's driveway, we didnt see a truck pulled over on side of the road with its hood up and two men lookin into it. Looked like old Jebediah Willie's truck, but we aint seen him there. Then these two turned and looked at us and one of em walked over to the passenger's side door and leaned in and someone must've been sittin inside the truck and handed that man somethin look like a gun. (We could just see a arm come out the window and then we seen that man put somethin in his pants.) Then he come back around to the front of the truck again and was sort of standin there waitin for us to get within talkin distance, but Pastor Varner closed his book and yelled to the man anyway from where we was.

Hello Brother.

The man was leanin against the front of the truck now, just lookin at us and smilin like he was a salesman or somethin. We all kept walkin, quiet again. We was a bit nervous, at least I was, and I couldnt take my eyes off these bright blue cowboy boots he had on. I could see em from as far away as we was. Them and his gun hand. People around here always apt to shoot somebody if they dont like what they up to. The other fella was still lookin under the hood at the engine, which was steamin a little bit. It was like a curtain of smoke behind this fella that was facin us and smilin at us so that he almost looked like the devil hisself was standin there waitin to block our way toward righteousness.

Hello Brother, Pastor Varner shouted again, and this time the man in front the truck raised his hand up, but with no gun in it (which was a good sign I thought), and then he waved but still didnt say nothin.

When we got close enough, Pastor Varner asked the man if they needed a hand, that he knew his way around a engine pretty good. The man said no, but ast us where we was headed.

Pastor Varner said we was headed to the gates of Hell, to walk into the fire, to rid our town of sin and human depravity once and for all.

The man in front of the truck laughed. His friend still hadnt even turned around.

Satan's ways are no laughing matter son. Have you yourself been saved? Are you a Christian?

No, the man said, still smiling, but I might be just the boy you're lookin for.

He spit on the asphalt and we all looked down and seen real good now those blue snakeskin boots he was wearin. The metal tips on em was scrapin at a piece of gravel that was on the road. Then he reached into the back of his pants and pulled out a pistol and placed it right against Pastor Varner's sweaty forehead.

Someone in the group yelled then but I didnt say nothin, didnt even move. I just grabbed my husband's hand and squeezed onto it. It's almost like I expected to run into somethin like this. Like how Pastor Varner always be tellin us that Satan be waitin around every corner to stop what is good and holy and righteous and it was our duty as Christians to snuff him out at every turn. He just aint never mentioned nothin before about the devil havin no gun.

September 3 1987

Tuck

As Tuck walked down Highway 16 toward home, the sky began to darken. Clouds rolled in and the tops of the trees were fanning the graying horizon like black and wiry paintbrushes irritating the sky with each gritty stroke. Tuck approached his driveway. He could see a group of people standing around an old pickup truck. The hood was up, so he couldnt tell what was going on, but he started walking faster. Then he heard something like a clap of thunder and couldnt tell whether it came from the sky or from the front of the truck. He stopped, put down his duffelbag, reached inside and pulled out his Colt revolver. He checked the chamber to make sure it was loaded, then put the gun in the back of his pants. He picked up his duffelbag and slung it back over his shoulder. Then he walked toward the truck and the group of people standing around it. Slowly now.

Pastor Varner

Lord God help me. For now I'm staring down the throat of death, the throat of Satan himself. Lord I need your help. This man before me *he knows not what he does* intends to shoot me leaving my faithful congregation to bear bloody witness, my lambs who shall be forever safe in the fold so long as they follow me O Lord. Give me strength to defeat this demon of Hell. To lift him from the flames and strike him down in order that I may continue to do Your work: to expel sin from our community for our crops and people, that they may be saved from Your wrath.

Lord God give me the strength to lead my people past this man, this demon, and to the land which has been desecrated by Sin and to those who are the cause of this blight. I pray to you Lord God that the sky may open up and cast this demon from before me, send him to the fiery pits of Hell from whence he came. Save me, save him, Lord God save us all.

In Jesus' name I pray Amen.

December 21 1987

Vermena

We could see him coming from behind the truck. I squeezed my husband's hand. He saw too. This son of God was coming to save Pastor Varner and likely all of us and we knew who he was too. It was Tuck Tucker, as if he'd done been brought back from the dead. He was edging around to where we could all see him clear as day but the old boy with the gun to Pastor Varner's forehead couldnt see him and that was just as good because I dont think he never even knew what hit him. Probably died tryin to figure it all out.

It all happened so fast but when this boy with the gun seen one of us lookin behind him he turned around right fast and that's when he seen Tuck comin up and Tuck just shot him without even thinkin or hesitatin.

It was the right thing to do.

Them two people in the truck (they was girls) went to hollerin and screamin but that other boy who had been at the engine went around to calm em down and we let him too since he didnt seem to have no gun or be interested in takin part in what his friend had been up to.

Pastor Varner fell to his knees as if in supplication now like we do in church and he raised his arms up to the graying sky, exalting it, his face splattered with that dead boy's blood, and some raindrops too if you can believe it, saying Thank You Thank You Thank You over and over again as if them words had never meant anything before that very moment.

September 3 1987

It had started to rain now, the drops small at first, just a drizzle, then coming down long and fast and pronounced against the dirt and rock and macadam. The people who felt it couldnt believe what was happening. And they stood in it, some of them for a good while to make sure it was real and not something they were dreaming.

The oldtimers in front of Shorty's stepped from under the tin overhang that covered the porch where they usually sat and they let the water wet their faces and their hats. The rain beat a steady rhythm against the rusted tin roof and snuffed out their pipes, which they relit when they sat back down, saying I'll be damned. Rightly came outer nowhere.

The folks standing around the dead truck whose hood was still raised and the overheated engine steaming with each quickening drop of rainwater looked up to the sky as if God had heard them finally and they could glimpse him there in the dark and gravid clouds overhead. Time had halted to a silent tableau. And everything was blanched with rain which began to pour harder and harder as the storm quickly rolled in from the west.

Joe

Joe Wallace on the tractor hears a gunshot now. It sounds close by, close enough for concern. He slows down, raises the Bushhog. Then the rain comes. Just like that. Suddenly and seemingly out of nowhere. He kills the engine. He walks across the yard through the rain, past the bloated horse which is covered now with a gray tarp but stinking and swarming with flies even in this rain still, for the ground, rock-dry, wouldnt take to a shovel for burying. And burning the corpse had been out of the question for fear the fire would spread.

Joe's shirt is darkening and his hair is dripping with the water. He walks up the porchsteps to where Magdalene is standing now, looking out toward the direction of the gunshot and looking at the sky and the dark rainclouds overhead. The rain.

Sounded like a gunshot, Joe says, shading his eyes with his hand.

Yeah, Magdalene says.

Think I should go see about it?

I dont know. Maybe it was just lightning.

I dont think so. It sounded like a gun.

Then I want to go with you.

I dont know if that's a good idea.

I'd feel safer with you than I would here, she says. In case it was a gun, and it finds its way here next.

Then let's get your rifle first. Just in case.

I dont want to get mixed up with any guns.

Just in case.

Okay, just in case.

Magdalene goes inside to get the rifle, letting the screen door smack shut behind her as the rain beats down on the tin roof.

Joe walks through the rain and across the yard which is already becoming a sort of swale now and he disconnects the Bushhog and he starts the tractor again, the water curtaining down the sides of the hood like clear plastic sheets. He drives it over to where Magdalene is standing on the porch with the gun and he pulls up and lets her place her foot on the back tire and climb on, keeping her feet on the running boards and handing him the rifle which he places across his thighs. He lurches the tractor into gear and they drive out across the yard, down the driveway and over the holes which are quickly beginning to fill with water.

Doyle

Travis is dead and I did not kill him. I dont know who these people are and who this man is that shot him but I know I did not kill him. I did not kill them either. I've never killed anyone. Yet God will kill me as sure as this rain that's washing over my face for all the trouble I've seen and likely allowed to happen by not killing Travis myself when I had the chance.

God help me make things right.

Tuck

Are yall okay?

Tuck is standing over the man he has just shot and he is looking out at the group of people before him, their drenched bodies wooden and statuesque in the rain. He puts his gun in his pants and he crouches over the body at his feet. He looks across at the man who is still kneeling before him: a supplicant. Tuck recognizes this man.

Pastor Varner, he says. Are you okay?

You are a true son of God, brother.

Huh?

You are a son of God, Pastor Varner says.

Tuck is quiet. He looks up at the crowd again, starts recognizing the faces therein.

Is he okay, he asks them.

That man you kilt was fixin to kill him, someone says.

What for?

To stop us.

From what? Tuck asks.

Doin God's work, someone else says.

Tuck looks back down at the body he has just shot, the eyes halfshut, black and swollen now from the bulletwound. A steady stream of blood coming from the ears, the nostrils, the corner of the mouth. The rainwater is collecting also in the opened mouth and overflowing onto the asphalt and then the purling ditchwater, bloody and with bits of skull and flesh and brain.

God's work? Tuck says. Hm.

Magdalene

As they approach the end of the drive Magdalene can see a group of people standing in the rain as if waiting for something. There is a broken down truck, its hood up, steam rising into the wet air as the rainwater boils on the hot engine's surface. She recognizes most of these people save for the two women who are sitting in the cab of the truck and one of the men who is standing next to them and who is talking to the women through one of the opened windows.

She sees Pastor Varner kneeling on the ground, as if he is praying, and next to him a body.

Joe, she says. Wait.

Joe stops the tractor and pulls the lever for the brake.

Oh my God, she says. The rain has wet her hair and strands of it are sticking to her cheeks and her neck.

What? Joe says.

That's him. That's Tuck. My husband. God, did he kill someone? What is this?

She looks ahead over the long hood of the tractor at the scene that has been laid out before them. She knows now that something is terribly wrong.

Joe says: Which one is your husband?

He's right there, she says. He's looking under the hood of that truck.

Joe stares through the rain.

Turn around, quick, Magdalene says, before he sees us. I think he killed someone.

Just sit here for a second. I'm going to see what's going on up there.

No, dont. Please.

It's okay. I have the gun. Something's wrong and I need to see what.

Magdalene is worried. She wants to leave, but not without Joe.

Be careful, she says, but Joe doesnt seem to hear her. He has already slid himself from the chair and taken the gun into his hands and is now making his way toward the road.

December 21 1987

Vermena

I knew it spelt trouble soon as we seen Tuck coming up to us with that gun and especially after he shot that boy who was fixin to shoot Pastor Varner. And then when it started rainin, I figured we was in for it soon enough. It just come out of nowhere. And just to prove I'd been right all along, here come Joe Wallace with a rifle in his hands and Tuck still under the hood of that truck finally looking up to see this stranger comin from off his land and then Tuck givin all of us a look like we had some explainin to do.

Who's that just got off my tractor with my wife on it? Tuck said to no one in particular.

Nobody said nothin.

Joe still was comin through the rain with that rifle and all of us just standin there waitin for somethin to happen. Miss Magdalene just sat there on that tractor not sayin nothin but watchin the rain and the steam come off the hood and the exhaust pipe and lookin at her husband and then Joe and then Pastor Varner and the dead boy and his friends and then all of us like she tryin to figure out what was goin on too, the steam steady comin up from the hood of that tractor and makin everything look foggy and like a dream.

Then Tuck moved away from the truck where he was standin and started walkin over to the driveway where Joe was, Miss Magdalene behind Joe on that tractor and it runnin still, the noise of it combined with the rain makin everything hard to figure out, hard to hear, like when I almost died givin birth to Darryl durin what seems like so many years ago now. But I could still hear Joe and Tuck talkin from where I was standin. They was right close by this point.

Who the hell are you? Tuck said.

My name's Wallace, Joe said, lookin at that dead boy on the ground, but not sayin nothin about it.

What you doin on my land?

What you aint been doin.

And what's that? Tuck said.

Tendin to things.

And my wife? What the hell is she doin?

Nothin. She's fine.

Is that so? Tuck looked back at the tractor, seein his wife sittin there but not even acknowledgin her. He looked back at Joe.

Joe said: Yep. Then he spit at the ground, his hair drippin all that rain and it all over his face and clothes.

I know bout you, Tuck said. I know who you are.

I know bout you too, Joe said.

I know you was up in Angola for them murders and that rape and kidnappin up in Saint Louis. I know what you done. I know damn well who you are.

Joe didnt say nothin then. He kept standin there in the rain. We all kept our eyes on him to see what he was gonna do, what he'd say. He put the rifle down. He said: I aint done those things.

Well I dont care. I just think it's time you went somewheres else, Tuck said. This here is my land you're on. And Magdalene's my wife.

If I leave, I'm takin her with me, Joe said.

Like hell you are.

Joe bent down and put his hand out for the rifle, which was gettin all wet now on the ground. But Tuck done put his boot over it, pullin out his own gun from the back of his jeans.

Not so fast, he said.

Then Joe Wallace, he done looked up at Tuck and that's when that boy who had been standin around the truck talkin to them girls and tryin to calm em down after Tuck done shot they other friend, the friend who was fixin to shoot Pastor Varner—that's when that boy grabbed Tuck's arm and pulled it back and wrastled that gun from it.

Wait, the boy said. Then he looked down at Joe as if he'd seen a ghost. He had been listenin to their conversation too.

September 3 1987

Magdalene

Magdalene is watching all of this from where she sits on the steaming tractor, but she cannot hear what her husband and Joe are saying. She sees Joe place his rifle on the ground. After a minute, she sees Joe bend down to pick it back up and she cannot figure out why he has done this, but then Tuck stops him and Joe looks up at Tuck and then Tuck pulling out a gun from the back of his pants and pointing it at Joe before Joe can pick up his gun from under Tuck's boot and then someone coming from behind Tuck and pulling the gun from Tuck's hand and throwing him to the ground so that he lands on top of the dead body and she can see the crowd that is standing behind Pastor Varner start to break apart and people running and she can see them screaming but she cannot hear them and then she sees Joe stand up with the rifle in his hand now but not pointing it at Tuck who is on the ground or this man who has just thrown him there but he is pointing it up at the sky and into the rain now where she can finally hear something which is the clap of the gun going off and she can see the flash it emits and everyone falling to the wet and puddling earth like trees being felled, calculated and deliberate and cold. And although she hasnt driven it in a long while, Magdalene slides into the tractor's wet chair and she puts it into gear and sets it forward through the mud and toward Joe, who is turning to face her now, his body streaming with rain and the man who just threw Tuck to the ground coming up behind Joe but Joe not seeming to see or hear him and Magdalene trying to yell over the engine and the rain for him to watch out but Joe only looking at her face and not at the man who is coming up behind him.

Doyle

Wait.

Doyle says this again coming up from behind Joe. He grabs Joe's arm. Joe turns. He's holding the rifle now. He points it at Doyle.

Dont shoot me. Wait a second. I done saved your life, for chrissake.

What do you want?

Did that man just say somethin to you about a murder? Somethin about Saint Louis?

I already said I didnt do it.

I know you didnt.

What? Joe says.

I said I know you didnt do it.

Good for you.

I know you didnt do it because I did. Me and him did. Doyle points to the ground at Travis, whose body is soaked with rain and blood.

Joe stares at this man, but does not lower his rifle.

We killed that man in Saint Louis, Doyle says, and we kidnapped his daughter and Travis raped her and almost killed her too. We done all sorts of terrible things, me and him. I read in the papers that you took the heat for it. I remember seein that. I know your face.

Joe is still looking at Doyle. Not talking. The rifle moves in his hands now as he takes this in.

I didnt do none of it really though. I was just too afraid to stop him. In fact, he just killed a man up the road a piece. Under that bridge yonder. You can see for yourself. This here's his truck we stole. It broke down on us right here. Talk about shit luck. We been in New Orleans the past twelve years hidin, and just recently decided to head somewheres else. We was on our way to Tennessee. Takin the back roads. But broke down here. Should've kept the car we was in. Like I said, shit luck.

By this point, Pastor Varner has stood to help Tuck from where he lay among the dead body and the mud and the rain. Tuck takes Varner's wrist and stands, wiping the rainwater from his face and eyes. He is watching Doyle and Joe now, listening.

Then Varner says: there is absolutely no such thing as luck brother. Not in this world.

And everyone as if set upon a stage: set into this twisted tableau as gears in a clock that have been wound and put into motion, watches the scene before them unfold as they hear from this man Doyle whom they have never seen before today that he is responsible for the crime for which Joe Wallace had been convicted some twelve years ago. Joe Wallace who has been living with Magdalene Tucker and who is pointing a rifle at the chest of the man responsible for taking those twelve years from him. Taking his family. His life. Everything.

And there is a man who is dead. Over whose body Tuck Tucker has been thrown, only to rise bloody and wet and angry, wanting to kill Joe now. And Varner and his congregation in the middle of all of this, having just wanted to rid their town of evil and sin which is what they are in the midst of now, they believe, and so Varner places his body in between these men, a lamb if he must be so, having helped Tuck up since Tuck had saved his life and everything beginning to move slowly, like in riverfog, as Joe thinks again of his years lost and Tuck thinks of his wife whom he betrayed and still loves. And Doyle thinks of the sacrifice he must make in order for things to be right again, that he must let this man Joe shoot him so that he may be cleansed of his sins.

The girls in the truck are screaming again. And Magdalene is sliding from the tractor now, not wanting her husband to kill Joe, for she loves him. Having never even known until now that he had been accused of any crime, let alone murder. She just knows she loves him now.

The rain continues to fall, washing away the blood from the macadam and onto the shoulder of the road where it seeps into the cracks of the earth and mixes with the water and the dirt and everyone standing and waiting for this to all be over so they can just go home.

Magdalene

Magdalene reaches out to Joe and gently pushes his arms down, the rifle aimed at the ground now instead of at Doyle. She tells him to come with her, back onto the tractor, so that they can go home, get their things, and leave this place for good. She has money in Mississippi.

Wait, Tuck says. Just what the hell do you think you're doing?

I'm leaving. As long as you're here, I dont want to be. You done left out on me and I'm through now.

And here I thought you was different, Tuck says.

I am, Magdalene says, turning her back to Tuck and walking toward the tractor, it steaming still in the downpour, which has not given even a hint of ceasing. Joe follows her, not turning, keeping his trigger hand on the rifle just in case, and looking the whole time at Tuck and his washedout clothes, who hasnt reached for his gun and doesnt seem to want to now but who is standing statuesque and defeated like he had just lost an important bout.

Magdalene steps up onto the tractor and Joe places his hand under her so that she can climb over the gearshift and onto the other side where she will sit on the slick wheel well and hold onto Joe's shoulder to keep her balance as they maneuver themselves over the muddy and desecrated road ahead. Then Joe places the rifle onto the running board, grabs the steering wheel, and pulls himself up and sits down in the chair and in a small pool of water that has accumulated there since they've been on the ground.

Pastor Varner

So here we are Lord. We have come to stomp out the sin from
our land and You have tested us and it is raining now so we have
surely pleased You. May the blight be lifted from here for good
now. For the sinners are leaving. Thank you Lord. Amen.

We have put Satan under our feet as it says to do in the book
of all books. And he is lying on the ground before us and we intend
to send him back from whence he came. I've asked my brothers
to help me put him in this broken down truck that once belonged
to Brother Jebediah who I had the privilege of baptizing when he
was a small boy, who You once saved from drowning in my very
arms for he did not know he had to hold his breath when I placed
him underwater such was the immensity of his faith, and to whom
I've ministered recently at his camp near the Bogue Chitto.

If Brother Doyle's confession is true and Jebediah has fallen
victim to this man who now lies at my feet, I ask you Lord to take
him into Your arms and to bless his soul. He is worthy. Lord I've
asked my brothers to help me put the body in this truck so that we
may burn it, the whole thing, rain or no, because I think it would

please Jebediah greatly to have known his truck became a vehicle by which Satan himself was sent from earth and back to Hell.

Lord I've never believed in luck. Or coincidence. Only Providence. Only You. I do not pretend to understand Your ways but I have an undying faith in them and in You. Amen. I believe we arrived here today, my congregation and I as well as everyone else, to banish sin from this town, to rout out the devil and his twisted ways for good. I believe that Satan tried to stop us but that you sent Brother Tucker to save us from him and to redeem himself for leaving his wife. And he's redeemed Lord. In my eyes he's redeemed now.

For Your will be done Lord: they are all leaving now.

This rain seems to want to last a while and our town and our people definitely need it and are grateful for it, as am I. Please bless us Lord today and on all days that follow. Bless us as we send Satan from us once and for all in this fiery oven we are readying for him. Bless us as we all make our ways home afterward. And let us be grateful for this rain, for this earth, for our simple lives and for this humble town: for it is good. All of it. Amen.

Joe

After they're settled Joe turns the tractor around, the eyes of those who've remained at the scene following his slow curving as if watching a painter's brushstrokes across a canvas, and he puts the tractor into gear and must hold the gearshift into place as he drives so it wont slip since the fork on the transmission has broken now after riding over all these potholes, filled with water now instead of the dirt they should be filled with, and he hobbles the machine down the driveway and back toward Magdalene's house, the rain behind them a curtain now, closing, blanching their image from the eyes of everyone and leaving only the two red dots of the taillights, becoming one now: seen only through the veil of water until the lights too are swallowed up by the trees standing on both sides of the lane so that there is nothing left at all except the sound of rain and the faint hum of the engine, struggling now with its burden of water and mud and its passengers jostled with every bump but hopeful still and looking ahead. Always ahead.

December 25 1987

Doyle

Me and some of the men from the church group had gone down to the bridge just outside of town after we put Travis's body in the truck. They wanted to see the man that Travis had killed earlier that day. Some of them seemed ready to cry when they saw the body but none of them did. It was still rainin real hard and we all stood under the bridge for shelter and Pastor Varner told me to dig a hole to put the body in and after a couple of hours when it was almost dark, and they had all just been sittin there waiting silently, I was finished with it and some of the men helped me wrap up the body in the tent and then we buried it and Pastor Varner said a prayer over it and everyone took off their hats and then when he was done, Pastor Varner asked me if I had ever been saved. I told him no but that I wanted to be, that I was ready for my sins to be washed away. He said that it was as good a time as any.

He had a couple of the men walk into the river with me and him leading the way and he opened his Bible and read from it as he doused my head with the water since it wasnt yet deep enough to put me under.

After that we all walked back to where the truck was with Travis's body in it. Pastor Varner had told me some of the women from his congregation had taken the two girls back to their houses to clean them up and call their families. I never seen either one of them since. Travis's body was in the cab of the truck and his whole head was black with blood and bruising and still wet with rain. Me and a couple of the men took off his boots and slung them onto the floorboard and then we went around to the front of the truck and we closed the hood and then we closed both of the doors and rolled the truck off into the woods as far as we could push it with the ground as wet and soggy as it was.

When we got it a pretty good piece from the road, one of the men opened the truck's door again and looked in the cab for some dry paper or something that would burn. He pulled out some papers from the glove box and told me to open the gas cap of the truck and to get ready to shove in the paper when he came with it. I did. And in a minute he came with his hand over a piece of burning paper that he had lit with a match in the cab of the truck and had wrapped around the end of a stick that he picked up off the ground and he told me to shove it in the fuel spout.

I shoved it in and then we all ran. Then the explosion came and we all plumb fell to the ground. We could see the huge flame and the black smoke at its ridgeline coming up through the trees and the rain, ravenous to burn all that was around it. We watched it, the fire eating its way through everything. We watched it and I couldnt begin then to understand its hunger. And I cant understand it now. A thing like that consuming both man and nature with such a sickening power is beyond me and for only God to sort out. I figure I'll let Him too.

David Armand was born and raised in Louisiana. He has worked as a drywall hanger, a draftsman, and as a press operator in a flag printing factory. He now teaches at Southeastern Louisiana University, where he also serves as managing editor for *Louisiana Literature*. In 2003, he won the D Vickers Award for creative writing. David lives with his wife, Lucy, their daughter, Lily, and their son, Levi. He is currently at work on his second novel.